The Gunfighters Law

First published in eBook
and paperback 2024

© Wyatt Steele

CW01497590

The Gunfighters Law

Contents

Dedicated to Ian Burnell

CHAPTER ONE

"Hold him still!" Jed Oakley's voice was sharp, a frustrated hiss against the dusty plains.

"I can't, Jed! He's wrigglin' like a branded steer," Slade growled, teeth clenched as he fought to get a good hold. Jed's knee was pressed hard against the man's chest, and his knife glinted in the midday sun, poised at the man's throat—a threat in steel meant to subdue rather than to kill.

The man, Ned, lay pinned on the dry, cracked ground, breathing hard as he struggled against the Oakley brothers' grip. His body twisted beneath Jed's weight, refusing to go quietly, each defiant kick sending up tiny clouds of dust that clung to the sweat on his brow. He was fighting for his life, and he knew it. His chest heaved as he bucked and jerked, each desperate thrash aimed at freeing his limbs. Jed's knife scraped close to his skin as he pressed harder, struggling to keep Ned pinned down.

"Keep still, damn you!" Jed spat, straining to hold Ned's arm in one hand while reaching for the rope with the other.

Slade, crouching near Ned's kicking feet, was just as determined. He gripped a loop of rough hemp rope, his fingers working quickly to cinch it tight around Ned's ankle.

"Quit kickin'," he sneered, though there was a twisted enjoyment in his eyes, watching their captive fight with every ounce of strength left in him.

With a triumphant whoop, Slade finally managed to get the rope's loop around Ned's ankle, pulling it taut with a vicious yank.

"I got him!" Slade's shout was filled with delight as he tightened the knot, making sure it bit cruelly into the man's skin. "Let him go, Jed!"

In an instant, Jed sprang back, letting go of Ned's arm and pushing himself upright, retreating as his brother finished the job. Ned's hands shot toward the rope, his fingers fumbling to loosen the binding, but it was too late. With a sharp crack of leather and a snort, the horse tied to the other end of the rope was spurred into a sudden gallop, and the rope went taut, yanking Ned's body forward with brutal force. He barely had time to cry out before he was being dragged over the harsh, uneven ground, his arms flung back as he fought to keep himself upright.

The world around him became a blur of grit and pain. His body bounced and jolted violently, his face scraping against the sun-baked earth, rocks and coarse gravel tearing into his skin with every brutal pull of the rope. Each jarring impact sent shocks of agony through his bones, and he could feel the sharp burn as his shirt was shredded, leaving his back raw and exposed to the unrelenting ground beneath him. He managed to turn his head, fighting to spit the dirt from his mouth, his throat clogging with sand and dust as he gasped for air.

"Stop!" he rasped, his voice barely audible, but the Oakleys showed no mercy.

He could hear the Oakley brothers' laughter from behind him, taunting and gleeful at his suffering. With a sudden twist, the horse changed direction, pulling him face-down this time, and he grunted as his right arm smacked against a rock hidden in the dust, the impact sending a searing jolt up to his shoulder. His vision blurred with the pain, his mouth filling with the bitter taste of dirt and blood, but he could still hear Slade's laughter echoing behind him.

"Keep draggin' him, Jed! Let's see if he's still kickin' when we've finished with him!" Slade said, howling with laughter.

Ned's hand clawed at the rope, his fingers raw and bleeding; each attempt to loosen the knot met only with more resistance. He barely had the strength to lift his arms anymore, and his back felt as though it were on fire, the skin torn and exposed as he was pulled mercilessly over the rough ground.

There was a brief moment of hope as the rope slackened, the horse pausing in its path to circle around. For a fleeting second, Ned thought he might be able to reach the knot.

But the respite was short-lived. The horse was spurred forward again, and this time, he was jerked with renewed force, his body spinning out of control. He felt himself veering off the road, his momentum carrying him toward a wooden fence post that loomed out of the dust like a specter. Before he could brace himself, his head collided with the post, a sickening thud reverberating through his skull. His vision went dark, and the last thing he felt was the cold rush of oblivion washing over him.

The Oakley brothers saw his body go limp, his hands falling slack as he dragged along the ground in silence. They slowed the horse to a stop, exchanging glances as they watched his body lie still in the dirt, bloody and battered.

"Looks like we done him good, Jed," Slade said with a grin, his eyes gleaming with cruel satisfaction.

Jed spat in the dust, his eyes narrowed as he sized up the unmoving figure in the dirt. "Ain't no point in draggin' a corpse," he muttered, dismounting from his horse with a rough sigh. "Get him off the road. The last thing we need is folks findin' him here."

They hauled Ned's bloody, lifeless form over to the edge of the road, dragging him to the top of a steep, dusty bank that sloped down toward the river. With a final, careless shove, they cut the rope and kicked his body down the slope, watching as it tumbled lifelessly, finally splashing into the river below, where blood blossomed in dark clouds around him.

Satisfied, Slade turned to Jed with a smirk, reaching for his revolver. "How 'bout I give him a partin' shot?" he sneered, cocking the gun and aiming at Ned's body as it drifted downstream.

But Jed slapped his hand away, knocking the gun from his grip. "Don't be a damn fool," he snapped, his voice cold and authoritative. "No need fillin' him with bullet holes. We want it lookin' like an accident, not a killin'."

Slade scowled, rubbing his sore wrist, his expression petulant. "Didn't need to hit me so hard, Jed. I was just having some fun."

Jed shot him a look of disdain, his lips curling in disgust. "Pick up your piece and quit actin' like a child. We got better things to do than waste bullets on a dead man." He turned his back on the river. "I got a thirst, and we're headin' to the saloon."

With a sigh, Slade stooped to pick up his worn, dirty Colt .44 from the grass, casting a last glance at the river as Ned's body disappeared around the bend, the blood trailing behind him like a dark omen. With a final shrug, Slade dropped his gun into the holster and followed Jed, laughing as they rode back towards Buffalo Gap.

CHAPTER TWO

Nash rode steadily along the winding trail from San Angelo to Abilene, the rhythmic clop of his horse's hooves echoing softly across the vast, arid plains. The sun hung high in the sky, baking the earth and casting a warm glow over the endless stretch of grassland.

He recalled stories he had heard about Abilene; it was a growing cattle town and a hub for drives and trade. Ranchers always needed hands during the busy seasons, and Nash knew he could prove his worth. It was hard work, but that didn't bother Nash. He'd happily exchange his labor for the sound of chinking dollars in his pocket. His boots, scuffed and frayed, were in desperate need of repair, the leather cracking and barely holding together, and he needed ammunition for the Henry.

Nash was a man happy to ride alone, but now and then, he enjoyed the company of others, and he couldn't deny that he felt a flicker of excitement at the thought of the bunkhouse that awaited him. It would be a welcome change – for a while. There would be laughter and music, and tales of their shared hardships echoed in the lazy melodies of the evening. There would be tales exchanged over the communal meals, tales of bravery, bragging, stories of impossible hunts and gunfights no man could ever win.

Company was like a good meal, Nash always felt, once you'd had your fill, it was time to move on. Too much was just bad for you. He'd enjoy it, be a part of it, and he'd know himself when it would be time to leave.

He'd work for a few weeks, just as long as he needed to, he didn't mind. Then, when he'd had enough, he'd head out of Abilene. He had no notion yet where he'd go, but something usually pointed him in one direction or another. Nash just liked to be moving, it didn't really matter where to, just on the trail, the scenery changing, his nights under the stars. He was more than at home under the open sky; if some men felt the loneliness of the plains, Nash didn't. His own company and that of the buckskin were enough.

As the sun dipped low, heading towards the dark horizon, the last ray sent a warm glow to stretch out across the vast prairie, Nash rode steadily across the open land. His buckskin tripped on a rock, and Nash knew immediately that a shoe had come loose. With a gentle nudge, he coaxed his mare to a halt. Dismounting with practiced ease, Nash felt the familiar creak of his saddle as he slid to the ground. He patted the mare affectionately on the neck, and the horse shifted uneasily, favoring one leg.

Kneeling down beside her, Nash carefully examined the animal's front leg. He discovered a loose horseshoe, its nails almost completely worn through.

"Well, girl, I guess you're just tryin' to tell me you're trail weary as well," Nash said resignedly as he examined the shoe.

The buckskin hadn't cast it; it remained in place, but the nails had pulled loose, and one side of the metal ring hung slightly away from the hoof. It couldn't stop like that. Nash pulled his pack from the back of the horse and found what he needed. It was a handy tool he'd been given by a smith a while back, flattened on one end and pointed on the other. Nash slid it between the loose shoe and the hoof and began to gently lift the shoe away, the nails coming out as well, their heads captured by the iron ring. All except one. One had sheared off clean with the hoof, the head broken away, the iron nail still embedded in the hoof.

"It's not good, girl, not at all. We need that nail out clean," Nash straightened from his work, letting the mare lower her leg down again, and stretching his back out, he let his eyes rest on the trail ahead.

Buffalo Gap was between where he was now and Abilene, just after it was the town of the same name. He'd head there. It took him a way off the trail, but not far, and the nail needed removing and the shoe reattaching.

"Don't you worry, partner. We'll get this fixed up in no time," he murmured, smoothing a hand down the mare's neck.

The fading sunlight painted their silhouettes against the sprawling landscape. For the remainder of the day, his horse carried only his pack, and Nash walked next to her. He didn't mind that the journey was going to take longer; he had no great desire to start working as a hand on one of the cattle ranches. If it took a few more days to get there, that was just fine by him.

The morning sun was just breaking over the town of Buffalo Gap, casting a warm, golden light over the dusty street as Nash walked in, leading the buckskin. The mare moved carefully, her gait uneven, dust rose up in small, swirling clouds with every step. The sound of clattering metal echoed softly in the stillness; it was the noise of a farrier's workshop, and he headed towards the sound. As he walked down the street, Nash's gaze took in the quiet buildings, their facades faded and weatherworn, each telling a story of a once-bustling frontier town that seemed to be sinking into silence. He'd seen plenty more like it. Buffalo Gap had had its day.

As they neared the farrier's workshop, Nash inhaled the unmistakable scent of hot iron. He could hear the rhythmic hammering inside, a steady metallic clink that broke the quiet morning. Nash stepped up to the open doorway, watching the farrier, a broad-shouldered man with a thick beard and a leather apron, busy at his workbench, sweat glistening on his forehead.

The farrier glanced up, pausing mid-swing, his gaze assessing as he took in Nash and the limping buckskin. He wiped the back of his hand across his brow and greeted Nash with a slight nod.

"Mornin', cowboy. What brings you my way?" His eyes flicked to the mare, he'd noticed the horse favoring her left front hoof.

"She's got a broken off nail in her hoof, didn't come out clean when I took the shoe off. It happened yesterday. I thought I'd better get her looked at before it worsens," Nash said, tipping his hat in greeting.

The farrier nodded his expression one of understanding. "The name's Hank," he said, extending a rough, calloused hand.

Nash took it, feeling the strength in Hank's grip, the handshake of a man who'd worked hard all his life. "Name's Nash. Mighty obliged to you for lookin' at her right away."

"Ain't got much else on this mornin'," Hank replied, a hint of a smile lifting the corners of his mouth. "Not many folks passin' through Buffalo Gap these days, not like it used to be."

Nash led the buckskin forward as Hank motioned for him to bring her closer. His gaze was steady and reassuring as he knelt down to inspect the hoof. Nash held the mare's halter, whispering to her in low tones, running a calming hand over her neck as she shifted, her discomfort evident.

"Easy now, girl. Just a little while longer," he murmured, his voice low and soothing. The mare snorted softly, her eyes reflecting a quiet trust as Hank carefully lifted her hoof.

"Well, there's your culprit," Hank muttered, examining the embedded nail with a practiced eye. "But I've seen worse. Nothin' I can't handle." His voice was calm, each word

16

like the steady swing of a hammer. Hank reached for his tools, the metallic clink of tongs and a hoof pick filling the air as he set to work, his hands moving with the confidence of experience.

Nash watched Hank intently, feeling a sense of relief as he observed the farrier's skillful movements. Each tool was carefully applied with the precision of a man who'd spent a lifetime at his trade. The mare flinched as Hank pried the nail loose, but she settled quickly under Nash's steadying hand, his quiet words reassuring her.

"There we go," Hank grunted, finally pulling the nail free and tossing it aside with a satisfied grunt. He inspected the hoof, ensuring no fragments remained, then nodded approvingly. "She'll be fine; she just needs a bit of rest. I'll leave the shoe off for now—give her a few days, and she'll be back to her old self."

Nash let out a small sigh of relief, a genuine smile breaking across his face. "Much obliged, Hank. You've saved us some trouble."

"Happy to help," Hank replied, wiping his brow again as he stood. "You'll be needin' a place to stay while she rests, I reckon?" He looked at Nash with a hint of expectation.

Nash considered it, nodding slowly. "Seems like a good idea. Got any recommendations?"

Hank smiled, nodding toward a building farther up the street. "The best place for a meal and a bed would be the Buffalo Gap Saloon. Belongs to my brother, Callum. He'll treat you fair."

"Thanks, Hank," Nash said, patting his mare's neck. "I'll head on over."

Leaving the mare with Hank, Nash walked up the street toward the saloon, his boots stirring up dust as he went. The saloon stood with an air of faded grandeur, its wooden exterior weathered by years of harsh sun and biting winds. He pushed open the door, the creak of the hinges breaking the eerie stillness inside. The room was dim, the only light was that filtering through the dusty windows, casting a warm glow over the empty tables and chairs scattered around the room.

The Buffalo Gap Saloon had once been the heart of the town, and the signs of its former life lingered in every corner. The bar, a long stretch of polished mahogany, gleamed with the wear of countless hands and elbows, lined with empty bottles that caught the light in muted reflections. Behind it, shelves held a collection of dusty glassware, each piece coated with a fine layer of neglect. The walls were adorned with faded paintings and some old wanted posters, ghostly reminders of the saloon's heyday, when card games, whiskey, and laughter had filled the air.

Nash took in the quiet, the room echoing with a sense of nostalgia that felt heavy, almost tangible as if the saloon itself mourned the loss of its past.

Callum, a tall man with greying hair and a friendly face, looked up from polishing a glass, his eyes lighting up with curiosity as he spotted Nash. "Well, howdy, cowboy! What brings you to Buffalo Gap?"

Nash tipped his hat in greeting. "Just passin' through. My mare threw a shoe, so I'll be stickin' around a few days while she rests at Hank's livery yard."

Callum nodded, setting the glass aside and motioning toward a narrow staircase in the corner. "Got a room upstairs if you need a place to lay your head. It ain't much, but it's clean. I'll show you."

Nash followed him up the creaking stairs, each step groaning under their weight. They reached a small room with a simple bed, a washbasin, and a single window overlooking the dusty street below. Sunlight filtered in through the glass, casting warm hues over the well-worn furniture.

"Looks good enough for me," Nash said, nodding appreciatively. It had been a long while since he'd slept in a bed.

Callum nodded and left the room; Nash followed; Callum locked the door and handed him the key.

Back downstairs, Nash took a seat at the bar, glancing around at the empty room. The quiet was almost unsettling, the kind of silence that felt thick with secrets and stories left untold. "Place seems pretty empty," he remarked, meeting Callum's gaze.

Callum leaned against the bar, a shadow of sadness crossing his face. "Aye, used to be busier 'round here. Back when the cattle drives came through, this town was a real hub—traders, cowhands, folks from all over. But times've changed. Big ranches started takin' their herds to Abilene, bypassin' us entirely. These days, Buffalo Gap's barely a stop on the map."

Nash listened, sensing the weight of Callum's words, pride mingled with a quiet resignation. "It's a shame, really. A place like this deserves better."

Callum sighed, pouring a drink for himself. "We're hangin' on, though. Folks 'round here are tough, even if there's fewer of us than there used to be. Got our stories, and we make do with what we got. But it's hard, watchin' somethin' you love fade away bit by bit."

Nash nodded, lifting his glass in a quiet toast. "Here's to holdin' on."

Callum raised his glass, clinking it against Nash's with a faint smile. "To the ones who stay," he murmured, his voice filled with quiet pride.

CHAPTER THREE

The first rays of dawn crept slowly across the little room, casting a warm glow on the rough wooden walls. Nash blinked, letting his eyes adjust to the soft light filtering in through the thin curtains. The mattress beneath him was firm but far more comfortable than the unforgiving ground he'd been accustomed to for weeks on the trail. He lay still for a moment, savoring the rare luxury, letting the stillness and solitude of the hotel room wash over him. It was a quiet, almost reverent peace, the kind he seldom found out on the plains.

As he stretched, Nash felt the last traces of trail-worn exhaustion lifting from his body, replaced by a contentedness he rarely allowed himself. For a moment, he simply took it all in—the muffled sounds of the town stirring to life beyond the walls, the distant clop of hooves, the creak of wagon wheels, the occasional call of a townsman beginning his workday. It was a marked difference from the usual dawn chorus of the plains: the gentle cropping of his mare's teeth against the grass, the buzz of early insects, and the mournful calls of birds. This was a place where life moved at a different pace, and Nash found himself appreciating the change.

A smile twitched his lips as he thought about the meal from the night before. Callum's wife, Marthe, had cooked a fine dinner, and he'd gone to bed with the satisfaction of a good meal sitting comfortably within him. This morning, he was already looking forward to breakfast.

He swung his legs over the side of the bed, feeling the cool floorboards beneath his feet as he pulled on his boots, their worn leather familiar and comforting. The floor creaked beneath him as he crossed the small room to the door, and he adjusted his hat before stepping out into the hallway. The scent of fresh coffee wafted from downstairs, mingling with the faint aroma of sizzling bacon, and his stomach growled in anticipation.

Callum was already bustling around the saloon as he descended the stairs, wiping down tables and setting out clean cutlery with an efficient grace that spoke of years of early mornings. The saloon's wide windows allowed sunlight to stream in, casting a bright morning glow over the rustic decor. Rough-hewn wooden beams stretched across the ceiling, and faded photographs of local legends hung on the walls, capturing scenes of cattle drives, gatherings, and the familiar faces of long-gone cowhands. The bar gleamed with the patina of years, each scuff and scratch a testament to the lively nights it had once witnessed.

Callum looked up as Nash reached the bottom of the stairs, offering him a warm smile. "Mornin', cowboy," he greeted. "Get yourself a seat, and I'll be right with you."

Nash nodded and chose a sturdy wooden table near the window, easing into the chair with a sigh. He could feel the morning sun on his face, the light playing over the tables, illuminating the dust motes that floated lazily through the air. A few moments later, Callum emerged from the kitchen carrying a steaming plate, a wide grin on his face. "There you go, cowboy. Best way to start the day in Buffalo Gap," he declared proudly, setting the plate and a pot of coffee in front of Nash.

Nash leaned back in his chair, taking in the spread before him. Scrambled eggs, fluffy, golden-brown pancakes stacked high and drizzled with rich maple syrup, and thick, crispy bacon lay before him like a feast. He didn't hesitate, taking his first bite of the eggs, which melted in his mouth, the seasoning just right. The bacon had the perfect crunch, the syrup added a delightful sweetness to the savory flavor, and the coffee was strong.

As he finished, he leaned back with a satisfied sigh, pouring himself the last of the coffee from the pot Callum had left on the table. In Nash's opinion, the best coffee in the world was the kind you didn't have to make yourself.

Callum chuckled as he came over to collect the empty plate. "I told you it was the best way to start your day," he said, his eyes crinkling with pride. "Want some more coffee?"

Nash tipped the coffee pot toward himself, frowning when he saw that it barely covered the grounds at the bottom. "That'd be mighty kind," he replied. "It's been a while since—"

He stopped mid-sentence as the saloon doors banged open with a violent clatter, the noise startling in the morning quiet. A woman stood in the doorway, her face pale and tear-streaked, her breath coming in harsh gasps. Nash recognized her from the farrier's shop the day before. She was disheveled, her hair falling from its neat bun, her eyes wide and wild.

"Uncle Callum... help! It's Ned!" she choked out, stumbling forward.

Callum's face fell as he rushed toward her. "Alice, what's happened?" he asked, his voice filled with concern.

Alice staggered sideways, clutching onto the edge of a table for support. Her voice shook her words barely a whisper as she finally managed to speak. "It's Ned... he's dead."

Callum stared at her for a moment, the shock rendering him speechless. Then, he tossed the cloth he'd been holding onto the table and sprinted toward the saloon door. "Alice, go find Marthe!" he called over his shoulder, urgency lacing his voice.

Nash had half-risen from his chair when Alice entered, his instincts immediately on high alert. He could see Alice struggling to stay on her feet, the strength seeming to drain from her limbs with every passing second. Releasing her grip on the table, she took two faltering steps forward, her face ashen, her eyes glazing over. Before she could collapse to the floor, Nash darted forward, his chair toppling over as he reached her, catching her in his arms just as her legs gave out.

24

The commotion had drawn Marthe from the kitchen, her hands still wet from washing dishes. She rushed over, taking in the scene with a gasp, her face filled with horror as she knelt beside them.

"Oh my, Alice! What's happened?" Marthe asked, her voice filled with worry as she placed a comforting hand on Alice's shoulder.

Nash shook his head, his expression grave. "I don't rightly know, ma'am. She came in sayin' Ned was dead. Callum ran out, and the poor woman fainted, I reckon."

"Ned! Oh my God," Marthe's words were choked in her throat, and she ran towards the still swinging saloon doors.

Nash looked down at the woman. His hold on her was awkward, and he wasn't quite sure what to do with her. Looking around, there were only chairs, and that didn't seem a good place to put a woman when she was out cold. One of the saloon windows to the left of the doors had a bench seat before it, and as that was the only place to take her apart from laying her on the bar, he carried her there.

Laying her on the wooden bench, he kept his hands close for a moment to make sure she wouldn't slide from it. Happy that his burden was safe, Nash headed towards the doors and peered over the top of the left-hand one. After all, it wasn't really any of his business.

Across the street was a worn-looking Conestoga wagon. The canvas top was missing, and the slatted boards on the sides were parting company from the frame. The back hung down, swinging below the wagon on its hinges. Nash could only guess at what was inside that the small gathered crowd was staring at. Callum was there, his arms around his wife, Marthe, her face buried against his chest.

And Hank.

The cry that left the farrier's mouth was feral with pain and anguish that could hardly be imagined, his head flung back, and his huge fists balled and held up in front of him.

Feeling like an intruder, Nash stepped away from the batwing doors back into the dark shade of the saloon. Whatever had happened was terrible but not part of Nash's life; he was tempted to take the last of his coffee and retreat back to his room. Leave these poor folk to their grief. Then he remembered the woman he had left precariously balanced on the narrow bench. It wasn't fair to leave her; if she woke, she'd likely tumble to the floor. So instead, Nash collected his coffee and moved to a table close to where Alice lay.

He'd barely had time to sit down and take a sip of coffee when the woman stirred, her hand raised in the air as if reaching out for support. Nash abandoned his coffee and knelt down before the bench.

"Careful, ma'am," Nash said, placing a steadying hand on her shoulder to prevent her from toppling to the floor.

Alice opened her eyes. Her face was deathly white, and her eyes didn't seem to focus, and she tried to lurch back upright.

Nash, an arm around her, helped her to sit up. "Steady, ma'am, I've been knocked out cold a time or two, and the worst part is coming back round. It's mighty confusing and turns your stomach sometimes as well."

Alice was quiet for a moment, perched on the edge of the bench, then in a rush, the reason for her faint came back to her. "Ned! I must go. I came for Uncle Callum."

"Your Uncle is across the street, and I guess your aunt is as well," Nash said, keen to retreat to his room with his rapidly cooling coffee, but instead, he asked, "Would you like me to take you out to them?"

Alice nodded.

Nash stood. "If you want, ma'am, it might be an idea to take my arm. You don't look too steady on your feet."

They made their way slowly across the saloon to the doors. Nash held the left one wide open for her, and they emerged into the light. Hank was now bowed over the wagon, his head hanging low. Callum still had his arms around Marthe, and he was rocking her gently in his arms, his own head resting on top of hers. The wagon, or more likely, its contents, had drawn men and women from their shops and homes as well.

Nash felt like even more of an intruder, needing to say something he said. "I'll take you to your father."

And that's what he had intended to do. Simply that. Make sure the woman, on her unsteady legs, made it safely across the street to her father. Nothing more. This was a family matter. Not his business.

"Alice!" Hank saw her coming across the street and stepped towards her.

Nash, thankful, took hold of the woman's arm firmly and prepared to pass her to her father and then return to his coffee.

Hank pulled his daughter close, then met Nash's eyes in the split second before he had a chance to turn and retreat, he said. "Look what they've done! You've been around, cowboy. Does that look like a man who's fallen into a river?"

"Well, I don't …." Nash tried.

"Just look!" Hank said, his voice harsh and filled with anguish. He pointed towards the wagon. They told me they fished my son from the river. The sheriff says it's the stones that have done that to him."

Nash hesitated. The coffee would be getting even cooler. He liked it hot, the aroma was stronger then, when it cooled it didn't smell as nice.

"Just look!" Hank demanded.

Reluctantly Nash stepped towards the wagon. The backboard was hanging loose underneath the wagon, and laid on the wooden boards were the remains of a man. His age was hard to determine. Threads of clothing still clung to the body where the seams were intact, but the rest hung in a tangle of flaps around the remains of his body. The skin was ripped, worn and ragged. Bloodless now after the cold kiss of the river water.

Nash swallowed hard. He'd seen this before. Seen such devastation wreaked on flesh, and it wasn't from the river. This wasn't

28

from the body being driven over the rapids in the water. This was much worse, and all those around the old wagon knew it.

"What do you think, cowboy?" Hank's voice gasped near his ear.

His coffee would be getting properly cool by now, there wasn't any point in thinking about it anymore.

Nash shook his head, not knowing what else to say. "I'm sorry, sir."

He knew the boy had been dragged. He'd seen it before. The skin was ripped and worn, and some of the wounds were still dark and impacted with grit from whatever he had been hauled across. Nash's eyes ran down the boy's remains to his feet and rested for a moment on his left ankle. That was evidence enough. The rope might have been cut away, but the gouge marks it had made on the flesh were still there.

"You saw that as well, haven't you, cowboy?" Hank had seen where Nash's gaze had rested.

Nash cursed himself inwardly. This wasn't his town. These weren't his people. And his coffee ... damn the coffee!

Nash knew he had to say something. There was an open plea on Hank's face: "Doesn't look like the river that caused this. I agree."

"You heard him," Hank turned to the townsfolk gathered around the wagon. Sheriff Hayes needs to investigate, and we all know who's responsible for this, don't we?"

29

Several men at the end of the wagon took a step back. Hank's mention of the sheriff was not welcome, it seemed.

"Who's with me? We can't let this go on," Hank pointed his hand around the gathered men. "Are you men?"

No-one moved.

"Alex, you've suffered enough, don't you want to stop those damned Oakley boys from running this town?" Hank fastened his angry eyes on a man standing at the side of the wagon, he wore a leather apron, sleeves rolled up to his elbows, and long sandy hair poked out from underneath his hat.

"I can't, Hank. You know I can't," Alex said, then waving a hand in the air, turned and walked away. "I'm sorry for you, Hank, and your boy. But I can't help you."

Alex's action was the signal to the rest of those assembled, and they, too, began to melt away from the wagon. This was a dangerous place to be, and no one, it seemed, wanted to be associated with Hank anymore. Fear was winning over their curiosity.

"Go on, leave, you damned cowards," Hank shouted after them.

A moment later, Nash found himself in the unenviable position of being the only man left standing next to Hank.

"Even this here stranger has more courage than you damned yellow bellies," Hank shouted.

This was not a situation Nash wanted to be in, but extricating himself from it wasn't easy. "I'm sorry for your loss, sir. I'll leave you with your family."

They were poor words, but what else could he say? Nash tipped his hat towards the women, kept his eyes away from Hank's, and turned before the blacksmith could object. He crossed the street back to the saloon and his cold coffee.

CHAPTER FOUR

Nash pushed the doors open and stepped back into the dimly lit saloon bar's sanctuary. Crossing to the table where he'd been seated, he took the mug in his calloused hands, the rich aroma of coffee wafting up to greet him. Taking a sip, he found it had turned tepid, and disappointment flickered across his sharp features.

Nash sighed, the mug resting heavily in his grip. With a resigned shrug, he raised the cup to his lips again. The bitterness of the cold coffee filled his mouth, a reminder of what could have been.

Nash went to his room, glancing out of the window before stretching out on the bed. He could still see the family in the street, Nash, Callum, their wives, and Alice surrounding the wagon.

Nash took another sip, trying to savor the coffee, but now it was not only cold but also bitter. Abandoning the cup on the side table, Nash pulled his boots off and stretched out on the bed. He didn't want to intrude on the family's grief. There wasn't a lot to do; his horse needed to rest, and he might as well do the same.

It was early evening before Nash descended the stairs from his room to the saloon again. The dim light inside contrasted sharply with the fading daylight outside. He scanned the room, taking in the familiar sights of the saloon—the worn bar, the scattered tables, and the dusty bottles lining the shelves. Callum was nowhere in sight. With a reluctant sigh, he made his way to the bar, where a few patrons sat nursing their drinks, faces cast in quiet contemplation as they exchanged murmured words.

The room was fuller tonight, weighted with tension, and the unsaid condolences hovered over the tables like fine dust settling in the dim light.

Behind the bar stood a man Nash hadn't seen before—an older gentleman, his face lined and weathered like an old trail map, with a grizzled beard and piercing eyes that held a quiet but watchful expression. As Nash approached, the bartender looked up, his hand pausing on the glass he'd been polishing.

"Howdy, cowboy. What can I get ya?" the man asked, his voice deep and steady, the kind of tone that commanded respect without ever needing to raise it.

"Whiskey," Nash replied, nodding toward a bottle on the shelf. Its amber contents glinted faintly in the light.

"Yes, sir," the old man acknowledged, reaching up to pull the bottle down. He set about pouring the drink, his hands moving with the practiced ease of someone who'd worked behind a bar for decades, each movement precise, measured.

As the glass filled, Nash considered the weight of the day, the somber news, and the sense of dread lingering in the air like an unwanted guest. "Is there anywhere I can get a meal?" he asked, his voice breaking through the haze of his own thoughts.

The bartender gave a slow nod in return, his gaze dropping to the bar as he let out a quiet sigh. "I'm Callum's pa," he explained, the weight of his words lingering in the quiet between them. "My wife, Nance, she's coverin' for Marthe while things settle. She has a good supper stew tonight—if that sounds agreeable to you, son."

Nash nodded, slipping his hand into his vest pocket and fishing out a few coins, knowing full well they'd be missed but not minding tonight. He placed them on the bar, an unspoken gesture of respect as much as payment. "I'll take some of that stew, sir, and if you don't mind, I'd like to keep the bottle."

The old man nodded, sliding the coins toward himself. His fingers briefly inspected their authenticity before he stashed them in his apron pocket. Satisfied, he slid the bottle across the bar to Nash, his weathered face softening with a hint of gratitude. "There you go, son."

Nash accepted the bottle, respectfully nodding to the old man. "Thank you kindly," he said. Then, after a moment's hesitation, he added, "And my condolences to you and your family, sir. It's been a harsh day."

The old man's mouth pressed into a thin line, his gaze dropping to the bar. When he spoke, his voice was quiet, edged with sorrow. "Sure has, cowboy. It sure has." He gave a brief, almost imperceptible nod as if he were gathering himself against the grief pressing down on him.

Nash took the bottle and walked over to a corner table he'd claimed before, pulling out a chair that scraped softly against the wooden floor. He poured himself a glass, the whiskey glistening in the dim light as it filled the glass, a rich amber hue that caught the eye. Unlike the bitter coffee he'd downed that morning, this drink had a certain allure, a promise of warmth and comfort within its golden depths.

The first sip was smooth, with a touch of sweetness, and the warmth traveled down, settling into his chest with a gentle burn, leaving behind a trace of spice. It wasn't the kind of whiskey that tore at your insides or stung your throat; this was the kind that invited you to take your time.

Around him, the saloon buzzed with quiet conversation, a murmur of voices broken occasionally by the clink of glasses or the scrape of a chair. There were more patrons tonight than usual. He wasn't surprised by the turnout. In his experience, bad news always drew a crowd. People came to pay their respects, to offer condolences—and sometimes to revel in the morbid curiosity that tragedy brought out in folks. Some stayed too long, overstaying their welcome, lingering over drinks they might otherwise have foregone, feeding off the tension like moths to a flame.

He glanced around, observing the patrons with a practiced eye. He saw the familiar signs of grief in their faces—the downturned gazes, the solemn expressions, the way they leaned in close to each other, their voices low, their words careful. Yet there was also a sense of weariness, an air of resignation that clung to them, as if they'd grown accustomed to loss, to the quiet devastation that seemed to befall towns like Buffalo Gap.

As the bottle dwindled, Nash's thoughts drifted to his horse. He wanted to go check on her, see how she was mending, and feel the reassurance of her steady presence. But tonight, it didn't feel right. He didn't want to run into Hank, not tonight. Tomorrow would be soon enough. He'd go early, take care of what he needed, and, if fortune allowed, have the mare reshod and be on his way by mid-morning.

He didn't care much for Buffalo Gap, truth be told. It wasn't his town, and it certainly wasn't his business. He'd come here out of necessity, not desire.

The sound of footsteps interrupted his thoughts, and he looked up to see Nance making her way over, a steaming bowl of stew balanced carefully in her hands. She set it down before him, offering a gentle smile that held more warmth than he expected. "Here you go, son. Hope it hits the spot."

Nash nodded, giving her a respectful smile in return. "Thank you, ma'am."

The stew was hearty, thick with chunks of tender meat and vegetables, the broth rich and fragrant, a reminder of the comforts of home. He glanced back toward the bar, where Callum's father was tending to the steady trickle of customers, his movements slow but efficient, each glass poured with a quiet dignity. Nash couldn't help but feel a pang of respect for the old man. Here he was, holding his family's business together, his grief buried beneath the steady rhythm of his work. It was the kind of resilience Nash understood, the kind that spoke of a life spent facing hardship and loss, not with complaint but with a quiet, unyielding strength.

As the evening wore on, the saloon grew quieter. Patrons trickled out one by one until only a few remained, their voices soft and muted. Nash poured himself the last of the whiskey, savoring a sip as he leaned back in his chair, letting the weight of the day over him. He knew his time in Buffalo Gap was nearing its end, and he welcomed it, the thought of leaving stirring a sense of relief deep within him.

Nash raised the glass to his lips again and let his eyes rove around the saloon. What men were left were scattered around the bar, their faces etched with a mix of anxiety and anticipation. Some leaned against the polished wooden counter, nursing their drinks, while others sat at the tables, their eyes darting occasionally toward the batwing doors that led outside.

Something was wrong.

The dim light cast long shadows, accentuating the patrons' furrowed brows and clenched jaws. A few of them fidgeted with their hats or adjusted the collars of their shirts, revealing the nervousness that lay just beneath the surface. Conversations were hushed, murmurs barely audible over the creaking of the floorboards and the occasional clink of glasses.

Nash took another slow sip. His eyes scanned the faces of the men. What were they waiting for?

Every so often, a man glanced toward the doorway as if expecting someone—or something—to burst through at any moment. The tension was like a coiled spring, ready to snap. In the corner, a poker game was in progress, but even the players seemed distracted, their eyes flicking up from their cards to gauge the mood of the room. The dealer, a wiry man with a moustache, shuffled the deck restlessly, sensing that the stakes had shifted beyond the table.

And Nash got the uneasy feeling that he was the only person in the bar who didn't know what was about to happen.

"Shift yer elbows, cowboy."

Nash looked up and found the old bartender there to clear away his empty plate and he leaned back in his chair.

As the old bartender, Walt, leaned over to collect the plate, his voice barely audible, he whispered. "The back door is open, cowboy. You might want to use it."

CHAPTER FIVE

Nash's fingers paused around his glass as he digested the warning. Walt's words weren't spoken lightly, and Nash knew better than to ignore them. His mother had drilled into him a saying: "Never ignore a warning, even from the wind." And here was a man giving him the closest thing to an alarm without ringing a bell.

Nash gave the old man a brief nod. "Thank you kindly."

He set his glass down, standing smoothly, careful not to attract attention. His movements were unhurried, his pace that of a man heading to the back for a casual stretch of the legs. He began to saunter towards the door that led to the outhouse, his shoulders relaxed, his steps deliberate. But he'd barely made it halfway there when the batwing doors at the entrance burst open with a loud thud. The heavy, solid step of boots echoed off the wooden floor, each step a grim announcement of the unwelcome visitors.

Nash didn't pause, didn't change his pace. He continued toward the back, but the murmur of voices that had filled the saloon dropped off, replaced by an uneasy silence. A feeling of exposure prickled down his back as he took two more steps. He could feel the weight of eyes following him, the tension palpable, everyone waiting to see what would happen.

"Where'd you think you're goin', cowboy?" The voice was rough, edged with authority and the arrogance of a man used to getting what he wanted.

Nash kept walking, his hand reaching casually toward his hat as if adjusting it. But the room was silent, and he could practically hear his heartbeat in his ears. He was close enough to the back door that escape was possible, but he'd have to be quick.

"I said, cowboy, where'd you think you're goin'?" The voice was sharper this time, brimming with impatience.

Nash stopped, turning slowly, his expression calm as he faced the source of the interruption. Standing by the entrance was Buffalo Gap's heavy-set lawman, his presence filling the room with an aura of intimidation, his status proclaimed by the badge on his chest. The Sherrif was a big man, broad-shouldered, his frame encased in a long duster coat that billowed slightly as he moved further inside. His wide-brimmed hat cast a shadow over his beady eyes, but there was no mistaking the look of satisfaction on his face as he took in Nash's halted figure.

The sheriff's badge glinted in the dim light, a symbol of authority. He stepped forward, his spurs jingling, each clink a sound of measured menace. The waistcoat he wore stretched a bit too tight around his belly, but the thickness of his arms, barely contained by his coat sleeves, spoke of a man who could handle himself. Behind him, two deputies had entered, both younger and armed, wearing expressions that mirrored the sheriff's

40

arrogance. One of them, with a scruffy beard and a deep scar running down his cheek, had the look of a man who'd seen his share of fights. The other was younger, his eyes darting around the room, betraying his nervous energy.

Sheriff Hayes let his gaze linger on Nash, a sneer curling at his lips as he took another step forward, the patrons instinctively drawing back. Those closest to the sheriff hunched over their drinks, keeping their eyes down, each movement showing their silent agreement that they wanted no part of what was about to go down.

"Well, well, what do we have here?" Hayes growled, his voice a low rumble that echoed off the wooden walls. "You're a long way from home, cowboy." He looked Nash up and down as if sizing him up. "Name's Sheriff Hayes. And I reckon you should tell me who you are and where you're headed."

Nash met Hayes' gaze without flinching, his expression steady, unreadable. He knew men like Hayes—bullies cloaked in authority, men who relished any excuse to show off their power. Nash could feel the eyes of the saloon on him, the tension almost electric, like the air before a storm.

Nash took a step forward, his voice calm, unruffled. "Just a man passin' through, sheriff. I'm here for a rest and nothin' more."

Hayes leaned in, close enough that Nash could smell the stale whiskey on his breath. "And while you're at it," Hayes continued, a sneer widening on his face, "you'll be handin' over your guns. No shootin' in my town, understand? We don't need your kind stirrin' up trouble."

Nash weighed his options, a flicker of irritation beneath his calm exterior. He'd known this town was trouble, but it looked like it was pulling him in deeper than he intended. Slowly, Nash let his gaze drop to the sheriff's hand resting near his gun, his fingers twitching with a readiness that spoke of countless showdowns before.

The sheriff's stare was unyielding, an unspoken challenge in his eyes. Nash knew he was at a crossroads: comply or resist. The saloon felt like a stage, with everyone watching, their breaths held, waiting to see what Nash would do.

"I'm not stirrin' up any trouble, Sheriff," Nash replied, his tone easy, his voice friendly, though his icy-blue eyes betrayed no warmth. "Just here for some rest and a meal."

"You sure about that?" Hayes drawled, his eyes narrowing. "Funny thing, cowboy, they just fished the Walker boy from the river this mornin'. I hear tell you've been fillin' his father's head with all kinds of ideas. That you have been encouragin' these good folk to think he was done to death."

Nash's jaw tightened, but his expression remained calm. He held the sheriff's gaze, his voice cool. "That's not what I said, Sheriff Hayes."

Hayes raised an eyebrow, a smirk curling at his lips. "Oh, really? So what did you say then, *suuuun?*" The sheriff's last word dragged out, heavy with mockery, the sneering tone unmistakable.

"I only mentioned," Nash replied, his voice level, "that his injuries were... unusual for someone who'd simply fallen in."

His words echoed in the silent saloon, each one resonating against the wooden walls, carrying the weight of suspicion. Hayes nodded slowly, shifting his weight, his spurs chinking with the movement. He looked down, exhaling a long breath before returning his gaze to Nash.

"Well, *suuuun*," Hayes sneered, the insult blatant this time, "it seems to me you've gone and stirred up unnecessary grief for a family that's already got enough on its plate. Accusin' folks in my town of murder? That ain't helpin'."

Nash's jaw clenched, his eyes narrowing. "I never accused anyone, Sheriff."

"Shut up, *suuuun*." The sheriff's voice was cold. "I hear you'll be leavin' Buffalo Gap as soon as your horse is ready. That right?"

Nash just nodded, keeping his expression carefully blank.

"Good," Hayes replied, his sneer deepening. "Until that time, hand over your piece. When you ride out, you can stop by my office, and I'll give it back. But not before."

Nash's shoulders tensed. He had no illusions about this man, or his deputies. They'd keep his gun, sure as day, and it wasn't likely they'd ever return it. But he knew when he was outnumbered, and the sheriff's hand hovered dangerously close to his own weapon. The entire room was holding its breath, every pair of eyes glued to Nash.

Nash raised his right hand, palm outward to show he wasn't reaching for his piece, and with his left, he deftly undid the buckle on his gun belt. He held it out by the buckle, extending it toward the deputy named Slade. A greasy grin spread over the man's face as he snatched the belt, eagerly examining the Colt as if he'd won a prize.

"Well, looky here," Slade sneered, turning the Colt over in his hands. "Sure is a fine piece, Sheriff."

Behind him, Nash heard the thud of boots on the stairs. The second deputy, Jed, returned, waving an old one-shot revolver in his hand, the wood grip split and held together by a crude binding of wire. He stopped beside Slade with a proud smile as he presented his discovery to the sheriff. "Found this in his room, Sheriff," Jed announced, his voice triumphant.

Hayes' lips twisted into a smug smile. "I think we're doin' you a favor, *suuun*, takin' that off your hands," he said, eyes gleaming. "Perry's don't even shoot straight."

The sheriff turned to the bartender, dipping his hat in a mockery of respect. "My condolences to your family, Walt," he said, his voice a smooth, insincere drawl.

Walt nodded in acknowledgement, his face impassive as he watched the Sherrif and his deputies leave.

"Come and sit back down, cowboy," Walt said. He'd rounded the bar and stood next to Nash, who was still watching the batwing doors swing after the sheriff and his men had left. Walt held another bottle of liquor and a glass, "And I'll join you if I may."

Nash retook his seat at the table. "Are you sure that's such a good idea?"

Walt pulled a chair across the floor, it grated noisily on the bare wooden floor and he seated himself opposite Nash. "Sheriff Hayes isn't interested in an old-timer like me."

"I kind of wish he weren't interested in me, either," Nash replied bitterly

"He's a sour man in the pocket of the Oakleys; both of his deputies are Oakley boys," Walt filled his own glass. "Those are the stupid two, their pa doesn't trust them with his cattle, so he has Sheriff Hayes nursemaid them for him."

Nash didn't reply. It was the same story he'd heard in a dozen towns. The law was local and exercised by those who had money. It hadn't been any of his business – however now they'd taken his pieces it was starting to look like it was.

Walt lifted the bottle and poured more whiskey into Nash's glass. "Old Pa Oakley is a mean cur."

Nash lifted his eyes and met Walt's. "It ain't none of my business, sir."

Walt grinned. "It sure is, cowboy."

"How do you figure that out?" Nash said, wishing the old man would leave him alone so he could retreat to his room. He had every intention of leaving Buffalo Gap tomorrow if his horse was sound.

"They've taken your pieces. You're not going to let them Oakley boys do that to you are you?" Walt said, then emptied his whiskey glass in a single gulp.

"Now who's trying to stir up trouble! I'm one man, it's not my town and now I've no guns either, what do you want me to do, stab them with this?" Nash said, a little annoyed and waving a fork that had been left on the table towards Walt.

"I was just sayin' that was all. No need to take offence, cowboy," Walt said defensively.

"None taken," Nash said, the tone of his voice saying otherwise.

Walt didn't say anything more. He drank a few more glasses of whiskey, and then Walt handed him the bottle, rose from the chair, and shambled back around the other side of the bar.

Nash, in no mood to remain in the saloon, under the gazes of the curious patrons, caught hold of the bottle by the neck and, scooping it from the table, headed towards the stairs that led to his room above the saloon.

CHAPTER SIX

Nash woke early the following morning; a bright slice of good morning sunshine was cutting through the partly closed curtains like honey, and he could feel the warmth from it across his face. Swinging his legs from the bed, he dressed quickly and pulled on his boots. When he went down the stairs into the empty saloon, neither Callum nor the old man, Walt, were behind the bar. He guessed that there was no one else up in the saloon, there were no smells of fresh coffee or cooking food.

Nash, close to the batwing saloon doors, looked out into the street. It was bright, and he squinted against the sunshine. The street was pretty quiet. To his left, a wagon drawn by a horse had just passed, and opposite, near Hank's livery yard, a dog was lazing in the dust. But apart from that, there were no other signs of life.

Pushing the swinging doors open, Nash stepped out onto the boards and dropped quickly down the three steps to the dusty street. He crossed quickly to the livery yard; again, there was no one around. The forge where Hank worked as a smith was cold, and the only noise came from the horses that were in the stables. They made soft sounds as they ate their fodder, the scuffling of their hooves on the stable floor, and the occasional swish as they battered the flies away with their tails. His buckskin was in the middle stable, Nash lifted the latch and let himself in.

"Hey there, girl, how are you doing?" Nash said, running his hand affectionately down the mare's neck. "How's that hoof looking?"

Nash continued to talk softly to the horse as he reached down and picked up the hoof from which the shoe had come loose. Running his hand around the front of the hoof, he thought it felt warm—too warm. Nash picked up her other front hoof, it was cooler. It was bad news; she wasn't ready to have a shoe put on yet.

Nash straightened and looked the horse in the eye, wondering what he was going to do. It was a good day and a half ride to Abilene, and he couldn't ride the horse. The alternative was to lead her in hand and find another smith when he arrived in the bigger town to fit a shoe. Nash tugged his chin thoughtfully; he knew it wasn't a good idea to take her on the trail with the shoe missing; it was a long walk, and he knew he'd risk her going lame. But then he didn't want to stop here, he wanted to get out of Buffalo Gap as soon as possible. It was a dangerous town. Nash could smell trouble and wanted to be no part of it.

He'd already lost one Colt and his old Perry, and he was in no doubt that the sheriff wouldn't hand them back over. That was a problem for later when his horse was shod, and his pack was filled with cartridges. Then he could figure out how he would get his pieces back -

48

because one thing was for sure - Sherrif Hayes wasn't keeping them.

"Howdy, cowboy." Hank's voice was friendly, but his voice told of a weary sadness.

Nash had been hoping to see the buckskin without running into Hank. After all, it was Hank's words yesterday that had brought the sheriff and his deputies to the saloon.

"Morning," said Nash, then asked, "When do you think she'll be good to get a shoe on?"

He knew the answer, but he still wanted to ask the question, hopeful that Hank might say something more positive so that he could get out of Buffalo Gap .

"I checked on her this morning," said Hank. "That hoof is mighty warm; putting a shoe on there now could lead to an infection, and she'll go lame in no time."

Nash nodded slowly, he knew Hank was telling the truth. "How long do you think it'll take before we can put a shoe on her?"

Hank tugged the beard on his chin. "I think you need to give her another three or four days, cowboy. If we put one on now, we could trap an infection in her hoof, and she'll be unrideable for a lot longer than two or three days."

Nash nodded slowly.

"I heard what happened in the saloon last night," said Hank. "I'm sorry for it, but now you know what those Oakley boys are like. Them and the sheriff own this town, they make the rules, they make the law."

Nash just nodded, it wasn't a conversation he wanted to be a part of.

Hank's anger was starting to rise. "I heard they've got your guns and taken them away and put them in the sheriff's office. I can tell you, cowboy, you're not going to see those again. I know what those Oakley boys are like."

Nash wanted to say that the fault for his loss of guns was Hank's; if Hank hadn't involved him yesterday, then the sheriff would not have come looking for him in the saloon, but he couldn't say that when the man had just lost his son. Nash was pretty sure his son had been murdered, so he swallowed his words and said instead, "I can pay you to keep her for a few weeks, and I might take to the trail on my own and go to Abilene. I'll come back for her in a while."

Hank, suddenly shocked by Nash's words, said. "You're just gonna leave?"

"There's nothing but trouble keeping me here," Nash said.

"What are you gonna do about your pieces?" Hank said.

Nash didn't want to talk about that, so he shrugged and saw the disappointed look settle on Hank's face. He felt he needed to say something, so Nash said, "I'm sorry, Hank. I'm sorry your son is dead, but I'm not the man to help."

Hank, muttering, turned away. "I'll keep your horse until you get back. I'm sorry we troubled you so much. I'll not take pay from you for her livery."

The morning air was still cool as Nash stepped out of Hank's livery yard and into the dusty street of Buffalo Gap. The light was clear and bright against the weathered buildings lining the road, and the stillness felt almost surreal. This town was tense, like a coiled rattlesnake ready to strike, and Nash could feel the weight of its gaze on him even if no one was out in the open. He had only made it a few paces when he saw Alice approaching, clutching a basket covered with a red and white cloth. The smell of freshly baked bread wafted toward him, a comforting aroma that felt at odds with the unease gnawing at him.

As she drew closer, Alice offered him a small, tired smile. Her eyes were red-rimmed, swollen with the evidence of recent tears. She stopped just a few feet away, her voice soft but warm. "Morning, sir."

"Morning, ma'am," Nash replied, nodding respectfully. He took in her fragile expression, wondering if the weight of all she'd endured would ever truly lift. "I hope the times ahead are kinder to you and yours," he added, the words genuine, his gaze steady.

Alice's eyes met his, and for a moment, he saw the sadness mirrored there, along with something more—gratitude, maybe, or a hint of resolve. "That's kind of you to say, sir," she murmured.

She stopped in front of him, adjusting the basket on her arm, hesitating as if weighing whether to offer him the contents. With a slight nod, she lifted the cloth, revealing three small loaves of bread, their golden crusts dotted with flour. The smell intensified, filling the air with a sweetness that made his stomach twist in hunger.

"There's nothin' much in the saloon for breakfast," Alice explained, glancing at the loaves as though unsure of her offer. "Would you care for one?"

Nash's stomach gave a low, traitorous rumble, but he smiled politely and shook his head. "They smell mighty fine, ma'am, but I've had my fill this mornin'." He lied, knowing that if he took one, it'd mean someone else, likely Alice herself, would be going without. His words were meant to reassure, but he couldn't ignore the pang of hunger as he looked at the bread.

Alice began to lower the cloth over the basket when both of them froze, alerted by the sound of hooves thundering up the street. Nash turned, watching as a rider approached, clouds of dust billowing in his wake. It was one of the sheriff's deputies, the one Hayes had called Jed. The man's approach was anything but subtle; he hauled his horse to a brutal stop in front of them, yanking hard on the reins. The animal reared, whinnying in protest as Jed slid off with an air of barely contained aggression.

He strode up to them, his movements exaggerated, swaggering, his eyes narrowing on Nash with thinly veiled contempt. Ignoring Nash, he tipped his hat at Alice, giving her a grin that revealed gums missing most of the front teeth. "What you doin' here, Alice?" he sneered as though she had no business in her own town. His attention shifted back to Nash, his eyes alight with suspicion. "This here stranger been botherin' you?"

Alice's gaze dropped to the ground, her shoulders stiffening, unwilling or afraid to meet his gaze. Jed's attention swung back to Nash, the hostile glint in his eyes making it clear he was eager for a fight.

"You scared the words right out of her," Jed sneered, then let his gaze drift to the basket in her arms. Without asking, he reached over, flipping back the cloth he grabbed one of the loaves. "Mighty fine smellin' bread you got here," he said, biting into it greedily, crumbs spilling down his chin as he chewed. "Best cook in Buffalo Gap, that's for sure. And you," he pointed the half-eaten loaf at Nash, "you've got no business talkin' to her, got that?"

Nash raised his hands slowly, palms outward, keeping his tone level. "I'm not lookin' for trouble. Just stoppin' by to check on my horse, and I'll be on my way shortly."

"Well, howdy, *suuuun*," came a voice dripping with contempt from further down the street.

Nash turned to see Sheriff Hayes approaching. His long duster coat flapping slightly as he walked, his thumbs hooked into his gun belt, his spurs chinked with each step, a slow, uneven rhythm that amplified the oppressive silence around them. Haye's face twisted into a smirk as he stopped a few paces away, his gaze raking over Nash with barely concealed hostility.

"What's goin' on here, Jed?" Hayes drawled, his voice carrying a lazy menace.

Jed glanced at Hayes, his mouth still full of Alice's bread. "Caught this drifter botherin' Alice, Sheriff. Figured he could use some… instruction."

Haye's eyes narrowed, and he took a deliberate step closer to Nash, his shadow stretching long across the dirt. "That right, *suuun*?" His tone was a thinly veiled challenge.

Nash met the sheriff's gaze evenly. "Just here to see if my horse is ready, sheriff. If it is, I'll be gone by midday."

The sheriff's lip curled, his eyes glinting with something dark and malevolent. "You'll be leavin' today, one way or another. I heard tell that mare of yours is pretty badly busted up—only good for meat, according to Hank. Fit for nothin' else."

Nash's jaw clenched, but he kept his voice steady. "She's not that bad. I'll collect my pack from the saloon, and I'll take her with me now."

The sheriff spat into the dirt, watching the fleck of moisture settle in the dust before he slowly raised his gaze back to Nash, his eyes cold, calculating. "No, *suuun*. You're leavin' that horse here."

Jed's hand drifted closer to his gun, his posture tense and expectant. The silent threat hung in the air, heavy and menacing.

At that moment, Alice shifted, stepping between Nash and the sheriff. Her voice trembled slightly as she addressed Hayes. "Sheriff Hayes, he weren't botherin' me none. Just askin' how we were holdin' up, is all." She lifted the basket slightly, a peace offering. "I've got some fresh bread here, sheriff. Would you like some?"

Hayes held her gaze, his mouth set in a thin line before he accepted a loaf from the basket. He tore off a piece, his eyes never leaving Nash's as he took a deliberate bite. "There's somethin' about you, *suuun*," he sneered, his tone venomous. "Somethin' that don't sit right with me. You're half-Indian, ain't you? Thought I saw that in ya."

Nash felt the familiar chill that ran down his spine whenever his heritage was thrown in his face. His expression remained impassive, but he offered a faint, polite smile. "If that bothers you, sheriff, I can't help it."

"It sure does bother me," Hayes said, his voice hardening, the loathing clear in his eyes. "Your kind can't be trusted, and we got no room in Buffalo Gap for half-breeds thinkin' they can stir up trouble."

Alice's face went pale. Her hands clutched the basket as she took another step forward, trying to shield Nash. "Sheriff, please. He didn't mean any harm."

Hayes took a step sideways, adjusting his position to keep Nash in his line of sight. "He don't belong here, Alice," he said, ignoring her plea. "Matter of fact, I'm thinkin' he stole that horse he's so set on keepin'. What do you reckon, Jed?"

Jed's mouth twisted into a nasty grin, his hand resting on the butt of his pistol. "I reckon you're right, sheriff. Looks like a thief to me."

Nash's eyes narrowed slightly, his gaze flickering from Jed to the sheriff. He kept his hands open, palms facing them, the gesture unthreatening but ready. "I'll pick up my things and go, Sheriff, no need for trouble."

Hayes took a step closer, crowding Nash's space, his face twisted in a smirk. "You'll pick up nothin', *suuun*. Your way out of town is that way." He jerked his thumb toward the edge of town, his voice laced with contempt.

Nash turned his head, glancing back down the empty street that would lead him out of Buffalo Gap. It was lined with ramshackle buildings, each one seeming to lean in, as if listening to the exchange with morbid curiosity.

Jed shifted to Nash's side, his hand hovering near his holster. "You heard the sheriff, boy. Get movin'."

Nash took a slow, measured step back, keeping his gaze on the sheriff and Jed. He didn't dare turn his back on them; both men were trigger-happy, eager to make a point.

"Alright, sheriff," Nash said, his voice low. "If that's how it's got to be."

Nash took three measured steps back, eyes fixed on the sheriff and his deputy, each movement calculated to keep his front toward them. He had no intention of turning his back and giving either man the chance to put a bullet between his shoulders. He wasn't alone in his caution; Alice seemed to sense the same danger. She shifted, stepping directly between Nash and the sheriff, her small frame a surprising shield against the tension bristling in the air.

"Sheriff, I'm real sorry if I've caused you any trouble this morning," Alice said, her voice sweet but with an edge of resolve. Her hands gripped the basket tightly as she held the sheriff's gaze. "I meant no harm, and neither did he."

The sheriff's face twisted, his eyes narrowing at Nash over Alice's shoulder. "Alice, this ain't your fault," he sneered, spitting in the dust. "This mutt here, half-breed like him, is nothin' more than a dog. And dogs, they bite. Can't trust 'em." His words hung in the air, each one carrying a mix of disgust and malice.

Beside him, Jed bit into another roll from Alice's basket, grinning as he chewed. He raised the half-eaten bread in a mocking toast. "Go on, you good-for-nothin' cur, get out!" he called, his mouth full, crumbs tumbling down his beard.

Nash didn't need a second invitation. Alice's presence had bought him just enough time. With a brief, steadying nod to her, he turned, his steps quickening as he moved toward the edge of town. The hairs on the back of his neck prickled with anticipation, but he didn't look back. Instead, he focused on the buildings passing by, each one taking him a little closer to the outskirts, each one a barrier between him and the sheriff's pistol.

As he passed the fourth building, the shouts behind him faded, but he could still hear Alice's voice, soft and calm, keeping the sheriff's attention on her. She was giving him time, more time than he'd expected, and he wouldn't waste it. Nash lengthened his stride, his boots kicking up dust as he neared the last row of buildings. He was almost out of town, almost out of their reach.

The voices behind him grew fainter, but he didn't let up, his gaze fixed on the open land ahead. The sheriff and his deputy wouldn't hesitate to put a bullet in his back if they felt like it. Only once he was beyond the final building did Nash allow himself to look over his shoulder. Alice's silhouette stood against the dusty street, her figure small but unwavering as she faced down the sheriff and Jed, her soft words shielding him from them.

Nash turned forward again, slipping beyond the town's edge and into the safety of the open plains.

CHAPTER SEVEN

Nash, his anger rising, kept walking along the trail outside town as it turned to the left. There was a small hill up to his right, and he clambered up the dusty bank and sat down, staring back towards Buffalo Gap.

Nash had nothing left, save for his hat and a few dollars in his vest pocket. Everything else he owned was in Buffalo Gap. His horse was at Hank's livery yard. If he'd had a chance, he'd have led her out of town and found somewhere where they could hole up for a few days, give her a bit more rest, and then walk to Abilene, where he could've got a farrier to fix the shoe.

That wasn't an option now. Even if he snuck back in at night and got to the yard, his horse was lame; he couldn't make a getaway on her, and the rest of his belongings were in the saloon room if they were still there. He doubted it would be long before Jed went to his room and claimed them. He always kept everything packed, you just never knew when you needed to move on in a hurry, so all Jed had to do was pick it up and take it away.

Nash found his way round to the river. It was shallow, and the water wasn't running quickly, certainly not quick enough to have stripped the skin from the boy's body he'd seen in the back of the old wagon.

The sheriff had been, in some ways, right. He was half Apache and half white, and he had been told in the past that this was a

59

better combination to outwit the sheriff and Jed. When night arrived, Nash had a plan of sorts. He needed to go back to the Buffalo Gap saloon and get back into the room that he'd been in. That was the start of the plan. Where it went from there, he wasn't too sure just yet.

Crouching down with his hands cupped, he drank from the river; it was going to be a long night. He wanted the town to go to sleep. He knew plenty of curious men would be drinking in the saloon tonight, wondering what would happen next. Shaking their heads and talking about the cowboy who had been cheated out of his guns and then his horse. They'd want it to end, want the sheriff to release his grip on Buffalo Gap – but what could they do? They had families. They had businesses to protect. They weren't gunfighters but shopkeepers, store owners, and wheelwrights.

Nash had heard it all before.

Sometimes he had some sympathy, and sometimes he didn't. This was the West. Sometimes, the only law was the law a man forged with his own fists and his guns. It wasn't a place for the unsure and the uncertain. He understood they had families, but sometimes you needed to fight to keep your womenfolk safe. It was just the way it was.

Nash, in the dark, was seated on a ridge behind the saloon, watching the drinkers make their way into the street. A little light from the oil lamps escaped around the saloon door and leaked through the windows. Nash waited. Eventually, the light went out.

60

Nash knew that Callum or Walt, whichever was in the saloon, had closed for the night, and the last of the patrons were gone. Slowly, he went down the bank at the back of the saloon to where the latrines were.

He stood in the dark behind them and waited, there was still a chance that some of the men from the saloon would've gone outside for a piss before shambling off home, and he didn't want to run into one of them. After a few minutes, Nash was satisfied that he was alone at the back of the saloon.

Walking quietly in the dark, he moved towards the back of the saloon. Would the door be locked? There was a good chance it would be. Nash put his hand against the door and pushed gently.

It wasn't locked on the inside as he had expected.

He kept on pushing, opening it slowly, trying not to make any noise.

"I've been expecting you," Callum said from somewhere inside the saloon. That's why I left the door open; I thought there was a good chance you'd come back."

Callum twisted the wheel on the side of the oil lamp, and the flame leapt, illuminating him where he sat at the table, sending shadows around the empty interior. Before Callum was a bottle of whiskey and two glasses.

"Drop the bar across the door, cowboy. We don't want to be disturbed," Callum said, pointing behind Nash.

Nash turned. A dark piece of wood stood propped next to the back door. Picking it up, he dropped it into two iron clasps, sealing the door closed from the inside—way more effective than a lock. Nash's eyes flicked to the batwing doors at the front of the saloon and found a similar piece of wood holding them securely closed. If anyone tried to get into the saloon, they'd get plenty of notice.

"Come and join me, cowboy," said Callum, pouring amber liquid from the bottle into the two small glasses. Then he slid one towards Nash. Nash picked up the glass, the liquid catching the reflection of the flame from the lamp. The whiskey smelt sweet, and setting the glass to his lips, he felt it sending a warming trail down towards his empty stomach. It wasn't food, but it was something.

"I saw what happened with the sheriff from the saloon window," said Callum. "I knew that bastard, Jed, would come for your belongings, so I hot-tailed it upstairs. I took what I thought you'd want and left the pack and very little else for Jed. Your things are over there in that canvas bag."

Nash turned in the direction that Callum had just gestured with his glass and saw the small bag propped against the wall.

"Got your tools, coffee, jerky, spare shirt, an' other stuff in there. I left Jed a blanket, your pack, and a pair of old boots, which I thought you could do without. He didn't get much," Callum grinned.

Nash raised his glass in a toast to Callum. "Thank you, sir, that is appreciated."

"The Least I could do. I'm sorry about your horse and your pieces. There's not much

I can do about that," Callum conceded and topped up their glasses again.

"Find anything else in the room?" Nash asked suddenly.

Callum shook his head, frowning.

A few minutes later, Nash was back in his room, Callum in the doorway watching him, with a confused look on his face. "There's nothing else here."

Nash lifted the mattress from the bed, and beneath it, lashed to the bedframe, was a Henry rifle, a Colt .44, and a leather bag of ammunition.

"Darn it, cowboy, that's not what I expected you to find!" Callum said as he followed Nash back down the stairs to the saloon.

Nash put the rifle on the table and spun the barrel of the Colt to check that it was loaded. Once he was satisfied, he put it next to the Henry.

"I got an old gun belt. It might be useful. It belonged to my grandpa," Callum said. He disappeared around the other side of the bar and retrieved something from a low shelf. When he reappeared, he was holding a dusty, yellow-brown, old-fashioned gun belt.

Callum brought it to the table, and Nash took it.

"It's not much, but you can have it."

"It's definitely better than the one that I've got now," Nash said, grinning at Callum.

The leather was a little hard, Nash picked up the Colt and slid it into the holster. It wasn't a good fit. Callum's grandfather's gun was probably a lot smaller than a Colt, it certainly wouldn't have been a revolver back then. At the top of the holster was a flap of leather that fastened down to stop the piece from coming loose. Nash had heard of them being called death straps; if they were fastened tight, then you couldn't draw, and even if they were unfastened, they could get in the way.

Nash fished inside his vest and found his last two coins. He put them on the table in front of Callum.

"There's no need," Callum said, raising his hands.

"I need to do what's right. That's just the way I was raised," said Nash.

Callum nodded. "And I was raised to provide good hospitality as well, cowboy."

Callum disappeared in the direction of the kitchen. Nash could hear the sound of the man moving around on the other side of the wooden wall. A few minutes later, Callum appeared with a tray. On top of it was bread, cheese, and cooked meat.

"It's not much, cowboy," Callum said, "But it'll fill your belly."

"Do you have a sharp knife and some oil," Nash asked.

Callum returned to the kitchen again, and when he came back, he put a bottle of oil and a cloth on the table, and from his apron, he produced a sheathed knife. "You mind the edge on that, I keep her sweet."

Both men sat opposite each other. Callum kept the glasses topped up and watched as Nash rubbed oil into the old leather of the gun belt. As dry as a desert, the oil disappeared as soon as it touched the leather. Nash kept on adding more, and the color of the belt began to darken as the leather came back to life, more supple, less likely to crack. With the knife, he cut away the death strap and then cut down the top of the holster, carving an arc out of the leather. He tried the Colt back into it again; the fit was better but not quite right. Removing the gun, he cut away another thin slice of leather. The Colt slid in better, maybe a little lose at the top, but it was a lot better.

Callum hesitantly asked, "What's your plan, son?"

Nash set the gun down and emptied his glass. "I haven't quite worked out all the details yet, but I know how it ends."

"How does it end, cowboy?" Callum asked, his eyes resting on Nash's face.

Nash grinned. "It finishes when I ride out of Buffalo Gap with everything I arrived with."

Callum smiled. "So you are going to go and see the sheriff the Oakley boys and get your guns back then?"

Nash nodded. Then asked. "Tell me about the Oakleys."

"There's old Pa Joe Oakley. He got his money from gold back in '48 at Sutters Mill in Caloma. Some say he cheated his partner out of his claim and then killed him, but I don't know anything about that. But he's a mean cur. He's got the Angel Ranch just outside of town, he runs it with two of his sons. The other two, you've met them, Jed and Slade, he lets the sheriff keep an eye on."

"What happened to Ned?" Nash asked.

Callum shook his head. "I don't know, and I doubt the Oakley boys will ever say. You've only got to look at them the wrong way, and they'll be firing lead at you."

"Jed and Slade, they come in here?" Nash asked.

Callum nodded. "Unfortunately, they do, every Friday night. Some of the boys have a poker game, and those two invited themselves to join a few months back. They never lose, and the rest of the men dare not win. If you look over there, you'll see the wood on the bar splintered where Jed started firing his gun off when Sam Senton made the mistake of putting a winning hand down."

"So they lose to keep the peace?" Nash asked.

"They do. More than they can afford every week," Callum shook his head sadly.

"Every week?" Nash said.

Callum nodded, took a long swig of whiskey, and shook his head. "None of them like the game anymore. Used to be a good time 'round that table, a few friendly hands and some laughs. But once the Oakley boys started comin', no one dares win."

"Well, that sounds like the place to start," Nash said thoughtfully.

"What are you thinking, cowboy?" Callum asked, leaning across the table towards Nash, hope in his eyes.

"I'm not too sure yet. Let me think about it for a while," Nash said. "It's three days until Friday."

Callum nodded. "Well, you can't stop here. There are too many eyes in the saloon, too many people coming and going. There's a loft over the top of the stables at Hank's livery yard; if you're willing, you can stop up there."

"Do you need to ask Hank?" Nash asked.

Callum smiled. "He'll be fine with it."

CHAPTER EIGHT

The sun in the western sky, cast warm golden hues across the dusty streets of Buffalo Gap, the town came alive with the day's last light. The wooden buildings, weathered by time and sun, lined the main thoroughfare, their paint peeling from the touch of the ferocious sun, but still vibrant.

Horses tied to a hitching post near the store pawed at the ground, their tails swishing lazily. At the same time, a few townsfolk lingered on the wooden sidewalks, exchanging quiet, guarded conversations. Alex Fisher swept the porch in front of his general store, the scent of tobacco and leather mingling in the air as he prepared to close up for the day. A sign creaked gently in the breeze, advertising everything from flour to firearms, the essentials for life on the frontier. The sun descended, painting the sky as a breathtaking canvas of oranges, pinks, and purples, casting a spellbinding glow on the worn wooden facades and glass windows.

Into this dying light stepped Alice, with the wicker basket over her arm and the checkered cloth in place. She crossed the street hurriedly, her eyes darting nervously left and right. She had no wish for another encounter with the foul Jed Oakley. She entered the gate at the front of her father's livery yard and headed towards the barn at the back where the horses were stabled, the sun casting long shadows on the path ahead.

The barn stood silent, its wooden doors slightly ajar. Taking a deep breath, Alice pushed the door open a little wider and stepped inside. She found Nash seated on a wooden crate, his hat tilted low, casting a shadow over his rugged features.

"Sir?" she called softly, her voice barely above a whisper.

He looked up, and a smile broke across his face, illuminating his strong jawline. "Ma'am! What brings you here?"

"I—I brought you some food," she stammered, stepping closer and placing the basket at his feet. "I thought you might be hungry."

Nash stood up, his tall frame towering over her, and reached for the basket. "You didn't have to do that, ma'am," he said, but his eyes sparkled with appreciation. "Thank you."

Alice smiled. "If you just leave the basket near the door, I'll fetch it later, sir."

"Nash, please, ma'am, call me Nash," he said smiling a little awkwardly.

"I will, sir, sorry, Nash," Alice blushed.

Nash looked away, sorry he'd caused her embarrassment. Alice looked as if she was about to leave, hesitated, and then she leaned in and gently kissed Nash on the cheek, a simple gesture.

"Thank you, Nash," she said as she whirled around and left the barn.

Nash, a look of startled amusement on his face, his hand straying to where her lips had touched his skin, watched her leave.

The meal was simple and delicious. Alice sure could cook, and he suspected he'd been given the best of what they had. Fresh bread, still warm, was a delight. Soft cheese, cooked meat, and an apple pie, sweet but still holding the delightful tang of the apples that it had been made with. When he'd finished, Nash dusted a few crumbs of pastry from his shirt and set the empty basket next to the door where Alice had asked him to leave it.

Returning to the crate, he began again the task he'd left off when Alice had arrived. He lifted the Henry rifle, its brass and walnut finish gleaming in the dying light. He hefted it in his hands and smiled, thankful he'd not lost it to the Oakleys. Nash ran his hands over the smooth wood and cool brass, for a moment admiring the beauty of the piece. Then, with his boot, he pulled a second crate towards him and set the Henry on top of it.

From the canvas bag, Callum had put his possessions into, he pulled out a soft cloth and began to clean the gun, making sure every speck of dust was removed. Next, he took out a cleaning rod, expertly running it down the barrel. When he was finished, he lifted the Henry, fitted the stock into his shoulder, felt the familiar pressure and looked down the sights on the barrel. Satisfied, he put the gun down and opened a bag of cartridges.

He'd had the gun a long time, had even had the pleasure of meeting Benjamin Tyler Henry. Meeting might have been too strong a term, but Nash had felt like Ben Henry had been talking directly to him, not just addressing a saloon full of men. He'd fallen out with the New Haven Arms company and in a bid to make a few dollars he'd a collection of Henry rifles to display and he was an entertaining speaker.

Henry was passionate about what he'd produced, and his force of will, as he had put it in his own words, persuaded the New Haven company to swap the rounds and change the lever action. It fired a .44 cartridge in a copper case, and he made the lever action smoother than southern whiskey. Each gun had its own pressure, and you could feel the exact point the cartridge was going to drop into the gun.

He'd hovered around when Ben Henry had finished and offered to help him pack away his guns. That was the first time he'd held a Henry, and his look of pure joy had made Ben Henry smile.

"Go on, son, put her to your shoulder," Ben had said.

Nash closed his eyes for a moment, savoring the memory. The feel of the polished wood, the gun's weight, the cold brass, and he could remember the smell; the rifle he held had not long since been fired, and it exuded that intoxicating tang of burnt gunpowder and oil. His own gun smelt more now of oil, it had been a while since she'd been fired.

He'd known from that moment that he'd own one. A gun that fired a .44 round and was capable of rapid fire was a formidable piece; back then, he'd only had his single shot Perry, and the Henry had shone brightly in comparison. He ran his hands down the rifle. There were dark nicks and dents in the stock and some deep scratches in the brass, but

Nash didn't mind; they were part of the gun. He'd bought it after the war from a Union soldier down on his luck, and it had not looked as it did now.

The brass tab on the side of the loading chamber had been stuck down so you couldn't slide a round in, and the spring behind it was fouled with dirt and old grease. The barrel was tarnished, and the wood was ingrained with dirt, and every part of the Henry's beautiful mechanism was stiff with neglect and misuse.

Cleaning it and reviving its beauty had been a joy to Nash, as had the first time he'd fired her.

Nash took some rounds and let them slide down gently, making sure they didn't slam against each other. Sometimes, he just kept a few rounds in her, but now things were different, and he slid in enough to fill her. The brass tab holding the rounds in place now was at the top near the gun barrel. Underneath, a long narrow slot revealed a line of bright brass cartridges filling the loading tube.

Nash liked this, a quick glance at the loading tube told you how many rounds you had in it, as each round was fired the tab moved down getting closer to the stock. He knew the rifle well, and knew exactly how many shots he had left. He didn't have many cartridges left, but there were still enough to fill the rifle.

The Henry was the first gun to give you a real second chance.

There was a sudden sound near the door, and his eyes snapped up, and he had the gun in his hand.

"I'm sorry, sir, I didn't mean to startle you," Alice said, she was leaning down to pick up the basket.

Nash put the gun down and smiled.

"My pa always told me never sneak up on a man when he's holding a gun, and I guess he was right," Alice said a little nervously, standing straight, the basket over one arm.

"Ah, so you were sneaking up on me?" Nash said, rising from the crate he'd been sitting on.

Alice blushed. "No, and I wanted to say, what the sheriff said about you being half Indian, don't bother me none."

"That's good to know, and it doesn't bother me none either," Nash said, grinning, then added. "I got the best of both, that's what my mother always told me."

"Was she Indian?" Alice ventured.

"Apache, and she still is. My name is Na'ashjii, it means little storm, but it's hard to say, so I usually get Nash, and I don't mind," Nash explained.

"What do you mean the best of both?" Alice said, she'd taken a few steps towards him into the barn.

Nash retook his seat. "Well, there are things the Apache are good at that white folk don't take to so well."

"What sort of things?" Alice said, sounding genuinely interested.

"Well, for one thing, the Apache have patience; they have a saying, that patience is the companion of wisdom," Nash said.

"That sounds like it makes a lot of sense," Alice said.

"It does. I don't reckon I've as much patience as my mother has, but I sure have more than most white men I've met," Nash said. "When you're not patient, a man rushes, and he makes mistakes."

"I hope you don't make any," Alice said, then regretting her words, the color rising to her cheeks she said. "I meant …. I'm sorry, I'm not brave, and I don't know what I am saying."

Nash rose and stepped towards her, his brow creased. "Ma'am, you're braver than most of the men in Buffalo Gap."

"Please don't say that," Alice said, taking a step backwards.

Nash wasn't prepared to let her go, not until he'd said his piece, stepping forward he caught her hand in his. "Ma'am, you stepped between a mean sheriff whose hand was hovering over his gun and me, that takes a special kind of bravery. Not one man in that saloon said a word when he turned up with his deputies and took my pieces, they could have, but they didn't. Since I got to Buffalo Gap you're the only person I've met whose got the courage to stand up to the sheriff and the Oakleys."

Alice's eyes met his for a moment, and she smiled, and then her gaze dropped down to the hand that he was still holding. "Thank you, sir … Nash, for saying so."

Nash gently squeezed her hand and let go, watching her as she left the livery yard. What he'd said was the truth. She was the only person he'd met who had any guts in this town.

Nash spent the night nestled in the cozy loft of Hank's weathered barn, the wooden beams surrounding him dark and solid, the scent of hay and aged timber filling the air.

From his vantage point, Nash could hear the soft rustling of the hay below, where horses shuffled and snickered. The rhythmic sound of a nearby windmill creaked and groaned, its blades turning lazily in the night breeze. Occasionally, the distant call of a lone owl pierced the stillness, its hoot echoing through the night.

In the quiet moments, he could hear the faint whisper of the wind as it danced through the cracks in the barn walls, mingling with the occasional flutter of wings from a resting barn swallow. The comforting sounds of nature, a soothing melody that lulled him to sleep. Nash, wrapped in the warmth of the barn, was content to listen to the world outside while he enjoyed his temporary hideaway. It wasn't the plains where he liked to sleep under the stars in the open, but he was alone with just the animals for company, and that was just the way he liked it.

CHAPTER NINE

The barn was dark, the smell of hay thick in the air as Nash sat in the shadows, his back against a wooden beam. He was waiting, listening for Alice's footsteps. She'd been bringing him food for the last two days. It was too dangerous for someone like her, but she didn't seem to care. Nash could hear her soft footsteps in the dirt outside the barn. He closed his eyes, waiting. He heard her light tread; he knew it was Alice. Nash smiled and stood ready, looking forward to the moment when she rounded the barn door, the basket over her arm, the checkered cloth covering the meal.

This time, he'd ask her to stop and share it with him.

Then, he heard a man's voice.

"Where you off to, Alice?" The voice slid through the air, low and slick. Nash didn't need to look to know it was Jed.

"Just takin' supper to my pa, Jed," Alice replied, her voice steady, but Nash could sense her unease.

Jed chuckled, stepping closer. "Now, that don't sound friendly. How 'bout you come here, darlin', give ol' Jed a little kiss, and I'll let you pass?"

"That ain't right, Jed. Leave me be," Alice's voice wavered.

Jed reached out, a slow, menacing grin spreading. "You're gonna be mine, Alice. Might as well start actin' like it now."

"No, Jed. Please—leave me alone!"

Nash's fingers dug into his palms, nails pressing so deep they drew blood. Hidden against the rough wood of the barn wall, he strained to listen, every muscle tight as he heard what was happening just beyond his reach.

"Just a kiss, Alice. Don't be so cold," Jed's voice was a twisted mix of coaxing and command, his tone making Nash's stomach turn.

A clatter sounded—Alice's basket hitting the ground. Nash could almost see her struggling, pushing against Jed's solid frame.

"Stop it, Jed!" Her voice was sharp, filled with fear, cutting through the stillness of the evening like a blade.

Nash tensed, his hand reaching instinctively for the gun at his side.

"Let go of me," Alice's voice was firm, but Nash could hear the fear underneath.

He could hear the scuffle, Alice struggling against him. The sound tore at him, ripping away the patience he'd been clinging to. His fists clenched the urge to burst out of the barn and put a bullet in Jed's head, overwhelming.

Nash's heart thundered in his chest as he hovered by the barn door, teeth gritted. His face to a crack in the boards he could see them both. Jed had her pinned against a fencepost, one hand gripping her arm, the other pawing at her dress. Alice fought him, slapping his face, kicking at him, but Jed just laughed, his voice slurred with drink.

"C'mon now, just a little kiss won't hurt."

Enough was enough. Nash had the Colt in his hand.

Nash's hand was on the door, ready to swing it open, prepared to end it all, when another voice boomed from across the yard.

"Jed!"

Slade. Jed's older brother.

Nash froze, muscles tight. He watched as Jed let out an annoyed grunt and looked over his shoulder, his grip on Alice loosening. With a sickening grin, he forced a final, sloppy kiss on her lips before stepping away.

"I'll be back later, Alice, an' you might want to be more favorable. You think about it," Jed sneered as he adjusted his hat, tossing a quick glance toward his brother before walking off, leaving Alice trembling by the fence.

Nash couldn't move for a moment, his heart pounding in his chest. He'd almost gone out there, nearly ruined everything. The Oakley boys needed to die together in that saloon. But still—he should've stopped it. Slade had brought an end to Jed's assault. Nash's hand relaxed on the Colt.

Alice was picking up the basket.

Her eyes immediately met Nash's, and she looked at the floor. "I'll just leave it here, sir."

Nash holstered the Colt and moved towards her. "That wasn't your fault."

"He might have found you," Alice's voice trembled as she stood back up.

"Well, he didn't," Nash said moving towards her

He stepped out of the barn silently, his boots barely making a sound in the dirt. Alice was still standing by the fence, her hands trembling as she tried to compose herself. She looked up when he approached, her eyes wide, tears shining in the moonlight.

"Nash..." her voice cracked, barely more than a whisper.

Without thinking, he pulled her into his arms, his muscular frame engulfing hers as she sobbed quietly against his chest. He held her tight, feeling the tremors that ran through her body, and guilt hit him like a hammer.

"I'm sorry," Nash murmured into her hair, his voice low, rough. "I should've stopped him."

Alice shook her head against his chest, her voice barely audible. "You couldn't, Nash. I know you couldn't."

She pulled back slightly, looking up at him with tear-filled eyes, understanding evident in her gaze. She knew what this was, what was at stake. Nash wasn't a savior. But that didn't make the knot in his stomach any less tight.

"I'll make them pay," Nash said, his voice hoarse with anger. "All of them."

Alice nodded, wiping her tears, her fingers brushing against the scarred leather of his vest. "I know you will."

Nash held Alice close, her small frame still trembling. Her tears had soaked through his shirt, but he didn't care. He tightened his arms around her, feeling her soft weight against him as if by holding her tighter, he could protect her. Her breaths came in ragged gasps, but the storm of sobs had passed, leaving only a quiet sadness in the air.

He didn't say a word. He couldn't. His mind was a tangle of guilt and fury, but words had no place here.

For a moment, neither of them moved, the only sound was the wind rustling through the barn and the distant crackle of the town beyond. He could feel her heart pounding against him, in sync with his own.

Then, slowly, reluctantly, Nash loosened his hold. He gave her one last fierce embrace, his hands pressing into her back as if he could hold onto her just a little longer, just a little tighter, before reality came crashing back in.

She sniffed, her fingers lightly gripping the edge of his vest as though neither wanted to be the first to let go. But he knew he had to.

With a heavy breath, Nash stepped back, his arms falling to his sides. The cooler evening air instantly filled the space between them, cutting through him like a knife. He watched her, her tear-streaked face turned toward the ground, her hands still trembling, and a part of him ached to pull her back into his arms. Alice looked up at him, her eyes red but fierce, and gave him a slight nod of understanding. No words were needed.

It was Friday. Tonight, things were going to change.

CHAPTER TEN

The saloon was always quieter on Fridays; just before the trouble started, no one wanted to be there when the Oakley boys showed up. Callum leaned against the bar, his eyes tracking the room, waiting for the usual crowd to shuffle in. He'd told Nash earlier that the Oakley boys usually came in to play poker on Friday nights, and tonight wouldn't be any different.

Dan Hardwood, the local wheelwright; Alex Fisher, who ran the general store; and Fletch McGrew, a ranch hand for old Hank, were always around the poker table. But things had changed since the Oakley boys showed up—uninvited. Big, broad-shouldered, and mean as rattlesnakes, the Oakley brothers didn't play for fun. They played for profit. Callum could see it clear as day, and so could the others. But none of them had the stomach to push back.

Callum put his empty glass on the bar, wiped his hands on the towel, and made his way to the kitchen at the back of the saloon. Opening the door carefully, he stepped inside. He stopped short. On the other side of the door, he found himself facing the dark barrel of a .44. Nash, seeing his face, lowered the gun. He wasn't alone in the kitchen. Marthe was there as well, an apron over her skirts. She was busy at the stove.

"You think the boys'll show tonight?" Nash asked, voice low and steady, his eyes narrowing in thought.

"They always do," Callum muttered. "They need that money. What they don't get through rustling cattle, they take from that poker table. But none of those poor bastards is brave enough to take a cent off them."

Callum stepped back into the saloon bar, leaving Nash in the kitchen. Nash's mind was already trying to determine how the night would play out. The Oakleys had pushed him too far. Tonight, they'd find out what it was like to push a man who pushed back. Nash didn't have long to wait; the Oakley boys arrived shortly after Callum left. The kitchen door was slightly ajar, and Nash watched as they seated themselves at the poker table, joining the other three men who were waiting nervously for their arrival.

"Those black-souled Oakleys have just arrived, haven't they?" Martha grumbled from where she stood in front of the stove.

"They have," Nash replied quietly.

"You can tell, the noise has dropped; every man stopped talking the moment they walked in," Martha lifted a pan from the stove and began to serve stew into two bowls on a tray.

Nash continued to watch the game.

Jed smirked as he dealt the cards, his confidence palpable. "You boys don't look too sure of yourselves," he taunted, leaning back in his chair. Slade chuckled darkly, his eyes narrowing like a predator sizing up his prey.

The game began, and the atmosphere shifted as Alex and Dan quickly fell into a pattern of hesitation. They played defensively, afraid to raise the stakes, fearful of the bad guys who seemed to revel in their unease. Each round passed with Jed and Slade winning hand after hand, their laughter echoing in the dimly lit room.

Marthe appeared, carrying a tray from the kitchen. On it were several bowls and thick slices of fresh bread. She made to walk past the table where the card players were, and Slade caught her elbow.

"What have you got there?" Slade said. He grabbed Marthe's arm, halting her and forcing her to lower the tray so he could see what she carried.

"I was just taking some dinner over to Hank and his wife," Marthe said nervously.

Slade grinned. "Well, you ain't doing that no more. You can make 'em some more. Put them on here."

Slade's stabbed the baize on the table with a forefinger rimed in dirt. "Come on, woman."

Martha obliged. With a look of hatred on her face, she banged down two bowls of steaming stew on the table, and then, with lightning speed, she delivered a hard slap against the side of Slade's face.

Jed hooted with laughter, the other players stared at Marthe, their faces pale.

"An' bring us more bread and another bottle of whiskey as well. Now git," Slade said, viciously shoving Marthe, who stumbled from the table and landed on her knees on the wooden floor. Turning to Jed, he said, "Looks like I got us some supper."

Jed reached across the table and pulled one of the bowls Marthe had left towards him. "You got more than supper," Jed said, still laughing.

Slade had his hand on the cheek that Martha had just laid her hand across. "When she brings me the bread and whiskey back she'll be getting a hiding."

The Oakley boys turned their attention back to the game. Jed took a card from the top of the deck, grinning and revealing his blackened, stumped teeth, added it to those he held and then slapped them down on the table. "That'll be my game!"

Grinning, Jed raked the coins towards himself. He'd not even bothered to wait to see if his hand was challenged. He knew it wouldn't be, and the other players around the table remained silent and kept their hands close. Jed's poker hand was poor at best, and it wouldn't have taken much to beat it.

Slade threw his cards toward Alex. "You, deal another hand. I'm a gunna win the next game."

Alex gathered the cards in with trembling hands, shuffled the deck, and fumbled them, spilling them on the table.

"You clumsy fool!" Slade declared and, raising a hand, slapped Alex round the back of the head.

The impact caused Alex's glasses to fall from his nose and rattle on the table, and he dropped the remainder of the cards he was holding.

Slade laughed.

Jed hooted and banged the table with his hand.

Between them a plate arrived, with bread.

Slade looked at it for an instant, then said angrily, "Where's the whiskey ...."

Slade didn't say anymore. When he turned his head to where he thought Marthe would be, he found that he was looking straight down the black barrel of a 0.44 Colt that was leveled at his head. Slade's eyes flicked from the gun barrel to the man holding it and locked with the blue ice-cold eyes of Nash.

Slade sat back in his chair. There was no fear on his face, just the arrogance of a fool. "So you're back, injun. You're going to regret that, ain't he, Jed?"

There wasn't a moment of hesitation, there was no chance for the players at the table to push themselves away. The barrel of the Colt shifted, lined up with Jed and fired. A 0.44 round drove a hole through his forehead. Jed was flung back over, taking the chair with him. His arms flew wide, and the gun he'd been holding and about to fire from under the table clattered across the wooden boards.

Nash didn't look at it. His attention was back on Slade – and so was the smoking barrel of the 0.44.

Slade's face was a mixture of shock and surprise; his hands had found the chair arms, and he was in the process of rising. The Colt stopped him dead in the act, his eyes on the gun, not on Nash. "You gone and killed him!"

"Seems so," Nash said coolly. Taking a step back, he smoothly dropped the Colt into the holster. "I got a question."

Slade didn't answer. The tip of his tongue protruded between his lips, and a crease split his brow – Nash knew exactly what he was thinking.

"I said, I got a question," Nash repeated the words.

It was enough to make Slade look from the holstered gun to the speaker's face. "What's that then?" He spat the words at Nash.

"Ned, Hank's boy, what did you do to him?" Nash asked, his voice steady and level was pitched so that every man in the saloon heard him.

"Is this what this is about? That damn fool boy?" Slade said, suddenly sounding confused.

"Just answer the question," Nash repeated.

Slade raised a hand and tugged his beard. Nash had already seen the bulge in the man's vest, and knew that beneath the leather was a gun, probably a short barreled, Derringer, and Slade was just biding his time.

"I don't know nothin' about what happened to that boy, nothin' do you hear me?" Slade roared; his right had left his beard and had lowered towards where Nash knew the gun was hidden.

"I'm sure you do, Slade, and ...."

Nash didn't finish his sentence. Slade's hand shot inside his vest, and he drew a piece from his chest holster. He got it clear of his vest, but that was it. Nash's gun was in his hand and he fired for a second time. The lead wasn't aimed towards Slade's head. Instead, it smashed into his right knee, sending a spray of shattered bone and splattered blood across the saloon floor. Slade dropped the Derringer, and his body contorting with pain rolled from the chair, and he landed heavily on his back.

"The boy, what happened? You got one knee left?" Nash said, the barrel of the Colt pointing to Slade's other knee.

Slade was rolling in agony on the floor, his face twisted with pain.

"The boy, Slade, you got two seconds," Nash said, and the entire saloon heard the Colt click. One more click, and it would fire.

"It was Jed, I swear …. he told the boy …. he was gunna take his sister and he got riled up …. and started punching Jed," Slade stammered between gasps of pain.

"So you tied him to a horse?" Nash said.

"Jed did, it was Jed, I swear," Slade mewled.

The gun that Slade had been trying to get from inside his vest was on the floor; reaching down, Nash picked it up with his left hand, keeping the Colt in his right trained on the wounded man. He knew it would be loaded, and when he stood back up, he fired it. The shot caught Slade in the throat, veins exploded, blood splattered across the floor, and Slade's eyes widened, his mouth open in a final gurgling scream that he couldn't make.

Nash didn't wait. He collected the Colt that Jed had dropped; it was the one he had taken from Nash, and he put it in the holster.

Rapidly removing one round from the Colt he'd used to kill Jed, he placed it next to the body, and the Derringer he'd used to blow Slade's neck apart with he put next to the still twitching body.

Nash stepped back. "Callum, I think you need to run for the sheriff. Looks like the Oakley boys have killed each other over a poker game."

For a second no one moved. Their eyes were fixed on the still body of Jed and the twitching Slade as the last of his life blood eked out onto the dusty wooden floor.

Callum was the first to move. "I'll get the sheriff."

Callum rounded the bar and ran towards the doors; a moment later, they were swinging in his wake.

Nash turned and ran his eyes over the men who remained in the saloon. "They argued over the cards, Jed said Slade was cheating, and he shot him twice before he died. Slade got off a shot and hit Jed between the eyes."

There was silence.

"You got a chance now. Take it. Stand up to the sheriff; he's one man, that's all." Nash looked at the card players and demanded. "What just happened?"

"Like you said, they argued; Jed said Slade was cheating ... didn't he, boys?" the other card players nodded, "then he fired at him."

"Nothing we could do, it was so fast?"

Another took up the narrative from the back of the saloon. "I heard 'em too, and Jed fired first, hit Slade in the knee, then got a second off and caught him in the throat."

"That's right, Slade had time for one shot before he collapsed," another said.

"Jed just went down, didn't know what hit him."

"There was no stopping them, it was over in a second."

"And the sheriff will blame you," Nash said, his gaze running over the assembled men. So, you'd better start acting like your woman folk and standing up, whether you like it or not."

The confirmation of the fight they hadn't witnessed continued. They were rid of Jed and Slade, and that was breathing courage into their veins for the moment. None of them even saw Nash as he disappeared through the saloon's back door and out into the night. They were still standing, debating the fight, surrounding the dead bodies when Sheriff Hayes exploded through the batwing doors, Callum hard on his heels.

CHAPTER ELEVEN

The saloon went deathly quiet, thick with the weight of violence. The acrid scent of gunpowder lingered, mingling with the stench of blood and whiskey, hanging over the room like a storm refusing to move on. Men stood around in stunned silence, their bravado drained as soon as Sheriff Hayes appeared. His heavy boots thudded against the wooden floor, each step punctuating the stillness as he surveyed the scene.

The sheriff's eyes, cold and calculating, raked over the two bodies sprawled on the floor. Slade Oakley lay in a pool of blood, his knee shattered, his throat torn open in a gruesome wound. His fingers were just inches from the gun that had failed him, the Derringer gleaming under the dim light of the oil lamps. Across from him, Jed Oakley lay flat on his back, his face frozen in shock. Blood trickled from his left nostril, and a dark, ugly hole marred the center of his forehead. His Colt was near his right hand, useless to him in death as it had been in life.

The men in the saloon shifted uneasily, sweat beading on their foreheads. Hayes stopped in front of the bodies, eyes flicking from Slade to Jed, noting the position of the guns, the scattered playing cards. To most, it would look like a simple shootout—a bad poker hand, tempers flared, guns drawn. But Hayes wasn't a fool. His jaw clenched, and his eyes narrowed, glinting with something deadly.

"Slade," he muttered under his breath, barely moving his lips, then turned his gaze to Jed. There was no sadness in his expression, no grief for his deputies—just a cold calculation. Slowly, he turned to the crowd, his gaze sweeping over the men in the room like a hawk zeroing in on prey. He paused momentarily, then his hand shot out and grabbed one of the men by the collar, yanking him forward.

"Alex Fisher," Hayes growled, his voice low and dangerous, the sound enough to make a man's blood run cold. "Tell me what happened here.

Alex swallowed hard, his face pale, his hands trembling. "S-sheriff," he stammered, "it... it looked like they killed each other. Over a card game. Guns came out... and then..." He trailed off, unable to find the words.

Hayes' grip on Alex's collar tightened, his eyes boring into him as if he could rip the truth from his mind. He glanced again at the bodies, studying the splatter of blood and the placement of the guns. Finally, he shoved Alex back with a sneer, his lips curling into a thin, humorless smile.

"You expect me to believe my deputies killed each other over a few cards?" Hayes asked, his voice as hard as iron.

Alex opened his mouth, but fear robbed him of speech. He just nodded, his eyes wide. Hayes scanned the room, his gaze lingering on each man just long enough to make them flinch. Then he knelt beside Jed's body, examining the hole in his forehead and the trickle of blood. Rising, he cast a glance out the dusty window toward the livery yard across the street.

"You're all cowards," Hayes spat, his voice dripping with contempt. "If I find out any of you are lying, you'll wish you were in the dirt with them."

Without another word, Hayes turned and stalked to the door, pausing just before he pushed through the swinging doors. He looked back, his eyes cold as death. "I'll find out who did this," he said, his voice a quiet promise, "and when I do, they'll pay with their life."

With that, he was gone, leaving a roomful of men shaken, each one knowing the real storm had yet to come.

Outside, Nash crept along the shadows of the saloon, skirting the town with practiced ease. He slipped through the fence around Hank's livery yard and made his way to the barn. He waited there, his senses heightened, listening to the distant sounds of men's voices from across the street, the creak of wagon wheels as they came to collect the bodies of the Oakley brothers. Jed Oakley was dead. Nash had put a bullet between his eyes, and it had felt good.

The noise from the street died down, and the cold and heavy silence in the barn settled around him. Then, he heard the soft sound of footsteps approaching, and his hand flew to his Colt, his fingers tight on the grip.

The barn door creaked open, and Alice stepped inside, her figure bathed in the pale moonlight filtering through the cracks in the walls.

"Nash," she called softly, her voice carrying a tremor he could hear even from across the barn.

He relaxed his grip on the gun and let his hand drop, watching as she approached, her boots crunching lightly on the straw-covered floor. She stopped a few feet away, her eyes searching his face, a mixture of worry and relief playing over her features.

"I... I just wanted to say thank you," she murmured, her voice thick with emotion. She looked away, her cheeks flushed, her hands twisting nervously around the edge of her apron.

Nash shifted, uneasy under her gaze. He couldn't shake how she looked at him or how her presence seemed to calm the storm brewing inside him. "You don't owe me thanks," he muttered, his voice low and rough.

Alice took a small step closer, her eyes meeting his. "I do owe you," she whispered. "You saved me." Her words were quiet but laced with a conviction that cut through the silence.

For a long moment, they stood there, caught in a charged silence. Then, almost without thinking, Nash reached out, his fingers brushing her cheek and lingering against her skin. Alice's breath hitched, her eyes widening as she looked up at him.

The air between them grew thick, fraught with something neither fear nor violence could sever. He leaned down, his heart pounding as he captured her lips in a soft, tentative kiss. It was gentle, hesitant as if they were both afraid of shattering their fragile connection.

Alice pulled away first, her face flushed, her breath shallow. She glanced down, her fingers fiddling with her apron, and Nash could see the mix of emotions flitting across her face—fear, longing, and something even deeper.

"I—I should go," she stammered, her voice barely above a whisper. She took a step back, her eyes avoiding his, and before he could find the words to stop her, she turned and slipped out of the barn, leaving him alone in the shadows.

Nash watched the door swing shut behind her, the warmth of her kiss still lingering on his lips. His chest ached with the sudden emptiness her departure left, an ache he hadn't expected, one that gnawed at him long after the sound of her footsteps faded into the night.

He stood there, rooted to the spot, staring into the darkness beyond the barn door. A part of him wanted to run after her, to pull her back into his arms. But he didn't move. He couldn't.

Instead, he stayed in the barn, letting the silence and the shadows swallow him whole, the memory of her touch lingering like a distant promise, one he didn't know if he'd ever be able to keep.

CHAPTER TWELVE

The morning sun cast long shadows over the dusty streets of Buffalo Gap, but there was nothing warm about the town today. There hadn't been since Sheriff Hayes' deputies had been murdered last night. Two men, allegedly shot each other in the middle of a card game —or at least that's what they told Sheriff Hayes.

The sheriff wasn't buying it.

Sheriff Hayes was a mean son of a gun on the best of days, but now, with the blood of his deputies staining the floor of the saloon, something had snapped inside him. He rode through town with a scowl deep in his weathered face, fists balled at his sides. The townsfolk could feel the tension building, like a storm that wouldn't break. Everyone knew the sheriff wasn't looking for justice—he was looking for someone to blame.

This morning, he'd started rounding up men, one by one, dragging them into the dirt by their collars, demanding answers, demanding names. And when he didn't get what he wanted, his fists did the asking.

Old Joe Miller, who helped Hank at the livery yard, had caught the first beating. Hayes yanked him out from behind a stack of hay bales and smashed his head into the stable door.

"You see somethin' last night?" Hayes snarled, spitting the words through clenched teeth.

Joe stammered, blood trickling from a busted lip. "I... I wasn't there, sheriff! I told ya before—I was mindin' the horses that night! Didn't see a thing!"

But that wasn't good enough. Hayes slammed a fist into Joe's gut, doubling him over, and followed it with another to the jaw. Joe crumpled like a sack of grain, clutching his ribs.

"Someone knows somethin'," Hayes growled, towering over him. "And if I gotta beat it outta every last one of you, I will."

He left Joe lying in the dirt and moved on, each stop leaving more blood, more fear, in his wake. Hayes' desperation was written in every wild swing of his fists. Whoever had gunned down his deputies had made a fool of him, and he wouldn't stop until someone gave him the answer he wanted.

At the general store, Alex Fisher tried to plead his case when Hayes came storming in. "I swear, Sheriff, the boys shot each other!"

Hayes grabbed the storekeeper by the front of his shirt and slammed him into a stack of canned goods. They tumbled to the floor with a clatter.

"Everyone in this town's got ears," Hayes barked, his breath hot on Alex's face. "You heard who it was. You know who it was!"

Alex shook his head frantically, his hands up in surrender. "I swear on my life, Sheriff, I don't know!"

But Hayes didn't believe him. Another punch, this one cracking against Alex's cheek, sent him reeling back. Blood sprayed across the floor as he hit the ground, groaning in pain.

By midday, the sheriff's knuckles were raw and bleeding, but there was no stopping him. He was a man possessed, more beast than lawman, consumed by his thirst for revenge. The town was paralyzed with fear. People locked their doors and prayed he wouldn't come knocking next. The ones who dared to peek from their windows quickly pulled back their curtains when they saw him coming.

No one wanted to be on the wrong side of Sheriff Hayes.

The few men who'd been brave—or foolish—enough to speak up against him found themselves nursing broken bones and busted teeth. Hayes didn't care. All that mattered to him was finding the man who pulled the trigger in the Buffalo Gap Saloon, and until someone spoke up, the whole town was going to suffer.

By evening, Hayes sat alone on the steps of the sheriff's office, his bloodied fists hanging limply at his sides, his chest heaving with ragged breaths. The town was quiet, too quiet. He'd beaten just about everyone he could lay his hands on, but no one was talking.

The deaths of his deputies weighed on him like a stone, but underneath that, there was something else. Fear. Whoever had done this was still out there, lurking, watching. And that made Sheriff Hayes afraid in a way he hadn't felt in a long time.

He spat into the dust, his eyes scanning the empty street. Someone in Buffalo Gap knew the truth. He could feel it, like a splinter under his skin. And until they came forward, this town wouldn't know peace.

Tomorrow, he'd start again. Tomorrow, the fists would fly once more.

It was Callum and not Alice who made their way to the barn next. "We got trouble, cowboy."

"We?" Nash repeated, then added, "Or more like I've got trouble."

"I'm with you, but the folks round here, they are ..."

"Yeah, I know ... where are they?" Nash said.

"In the street, Sherrif Hayes has taken off outta town," Callum said.

A crowd had gathered in the center of Buffalo Gap, townsfolk casting sidelong glances at Nash, muttering under their breath. Some faces were hardened with anger, others fearful, all turned against him in a slow, simmering wave of resentment. Nash stood alone, his tall figure stark against the dusty backdrop, his cold blue eyes surveying the mob with a wary and unyielding look.

Alex Fisher, his face bruised, lip split, stepped forward from the group, his face twisted with anger. Nash turned those icy eyes on him, sizing him up before he spoke, his voice low and steady. "No one wants trouble, but trouble's what we got. And you started it, cowboy."

The crowd murmured, shifting uncomfortably. Another man to Nash's right—a wiry fellow named Clem—cut through the quiet, his tone sharp. "You killed Jed and Slade, that wasn't us," Clem said, his gaze hard, challenging.

Nash turned, his expression calm, almost indifferent. "That's true," he acknowledged, his voice as steady as iron.

Clem pressed on, encouraged by the grumbles from the crowd. "And Pa Oakley and the rest of 'em are gonna be hot-footin' it over here when they hear. Sherrif doesn't believe that story either, and he's been using his fists all day. Broke Ted's jaw, and Alex Fisher's nursing a coupla' broken ribs because of you."

A few voices murmured agreement, heads nodding, eyes narrowing at Nash as though he were the snake that had slithered into their midst. Nash knew exactly what Clem was doing—stoking their fears, twisting the situation to make him the scapegoat. Clem's tone took on a sly, accusatory edge. "All this bloodshed, you bringin' it down on us. We were gettin' by just fine till you came along, Nash."

Nash took a step forward, his gaze cool but intense, his voice cutting through the murmur of the crowd like a knife. "You had to hold out against one man! There are a dozen of you here. Why did you let Hayes pick on you one by one? If you'd stood together, there would have been nothing he could have done."

"That's all fine to say, but it ain't you whose payin' the price. It'll be our homes, our families," one of the men in the crowd shot

100

back; he had a black eye, no doubt delivered by the sheriff earlier that day.

Silence hung thick in the air, punctuated only by the creak of leather and the shuffle of boots. The truth of his words lingered, but fear and anger clouded their judgment. The crowd looked to Clem, who wore a smug, self-satisfied expression, the flicker of a grin barely concealed.

"We don't need no hero like you, Nash," Clem said, his voice filled with venom. "You brought this down on us, and now we're the ones left to pick up the pieces. You best be gone by sundown, or we'll see to it ourselves."

Nash held Clem's gaze for a long moment, his expression unreadable. Then, he inclined his head, a slow nod of acknowledgement, as though conceding some unspoken truth.

"If that's how you want it," Nash replied, his voice low, a hint of something dangerous lurking beneath his calm exterior. "But when the Oakleys come, don't go lookin' my way. You made your choice." He turned his back on the crowd, shoulders square, and walked slowly down the street.

Behind him, the crowd broke into whispers, the townsfolk casting wary glances his way. Clem watched Nash go, his smirk deepening. But a few faces wore expressions of doubt, their unease growing, as if realizing, too late, the price of casting out the only man willing to stand up to the sheriff and the Oakleys.

Nash made his way back to the livery and collected his horse; leading it out, he tied her to a small hitching post, where his horse waited, head drooping. Nash gave the horse a long, steady look, running a calloused hand along its neck, murmuring low to calm it as he shifted his saddlebag and supplies onto its back. He'd walk with her to Abilene and find another farrier – Buffalo Gap could burn for all he cared.

With slow, practiced movements, Nash loaded his few belongings: a rolled bedroll, a weather-beaten canteen, and the Henry rifle strapped beside the saddle. He could feel the eyes of the townsfolk on him, watching from windows and porches, their whispers carried on the dry, dusty air. No one stepped forward; they kept to their shadows, silently marking his departure.

The only man who broke away from the crowd was Callum, the saloon bartender. His thick apron was still hanging from his neck, and he had a deep frown on his face. He walked up to Nash, looking back at the crowd as if half-expecting them to follow.

"You don't have to go, Nash," Callum said, his voice rough with worry. "They're scared. You know how folks get when fear sinks its teeth in."

Nash paused, adjusting his saddle, his cold blue eyes lifting to meet Callum's. "Fear's a choice, Callum. They chose to turn on me as soon as Hayes became their problem." His voice was low and flat, holding none of the bitterness Callum expected—just a simple, unyielding truth.

Callum's hand twitched as if he wanted to reach out to keep Nash from saddling up.

"You did right by them, Nash. Not everyone's turned against you. Some of us still believe in what you did."

Nash gave a slow, grim nod. "I appreciate that, Callum. But belief doesn't change the fact that they're ready to hand me over if it keeps the Oakleys off their backs." He tightened the saddle's girth, every movement steady, like a man who'd long since made peace with his choices.

Behind Callum, a few of the townsfolk lingered, watching silently. Their faces were wary, and their expressions a blend of fear and guilt. Not one of them stepped forward.

Callum's face hardened, but there was sadness in his eyes. "You know this town'll go to hell without you. The sheriff will rip it apart."

Nash gazed at the distant mountains, the wide, open plains stretching before him. "The stop him. Maybe it'll teach them that some things are worth fightin' for." He gave Callum one last nod and leading the mare headed out of Buffalo Gap. "Take care of yourself, Callum."

With that, he left Buffalo Gap, leaving the townsfolk to their fate. Not one of them raised a hand to wave, call him back, or even thank him. They simply watched in silence, their faces pinched with regret and fear, knowing they were sending away the one man who might have saved them.

Nash didn't look back.

CHAPTER THIRTEEN

Sheriff Hayes woke with a headache, the pounding in his skull echoing the fury that had settled deep in his bones. Yesterday had been a mess of fists and threats, and still, no one had given him what he wanted. His deputies were dead, gunned down in cold blood during a card game at the Buffalo Gap Saloon, and the entire town had closed its lips. He knew someone knew something. But no one was talking. Jed and Slade might have been stupid, but they weren't stupid enough to have killed each other.

By noon, he was saddling up, heading back into town with one thought on his mind: Alex Fisher. The storekeeper had taken a good beating the day before, but Hayes wasn't finished with him. Fisher was the weak link, he'd been at the poker table. He'd seen what had happened, and Hayes had seen the fear in the man's eyes. Fear was useful. Fear could break a man down.

The streets of Buffalo Gap were quiet as the sheriff rode in, the townsfolk keeping their distance. People had learned to stay out of his way when he was like this—wound up, dangerous. Hayes dismounted outside the general store, his boots hitting the dirt hard as he strode through the door.

Alex was behind the counter, his face still swollen from the blows he'd taken the day before. When he saw Hayes enter, his hands trembled, knocking a can off the shelf. He didn't bother to pick it up.

"Sheriff..." Alex stammered, taking a step back, his eyes wide with a mix of fear and dread.

Hayes slammed the door behind him, the sound reverberating through the small shop like a gunshot. He sauntered toward the counter, his boots heavy on the floorboards, his eyes locked on Alex.

"Yesterday," Hayes growled, his voice low and dangerous, "you told me you didn't know nothin' about what happened in that saloon. I'm here to see if you've had a change of heart."

Alex swallowed hard, his throat dry. He'd been expecting this, but no amount of preparation had steadied his nerves. His heart pounded in his chest like a runaway horse.

"Sheriff, I—" Alex's voice cracked, and he wiped the sweat from his brow. "I told you everything I know."

Hayes was across the room in two strides, grabbing Alex by the front of his shirt and hauling him over the counter. He slammed the man into a shelf of goods, knocking jars and cans to the floor in a clattering mess.

"You're lyin'!" Hayes snarled, his fist raised. "And if I gotta beat the truth out of you, I will. What happened to my men?"

Alex's face went pale, his lip trembling. He couldn't hold out any longer.

"It was that cowboy!" Alex blurted, his voice high with panic. "The one you ran outta town! The one you robbed of his guns!"

Hayes froze his fist still in the air. His grip loosened on Alex's shirt as the words sank in. That cowboy... The one he'd humiliated a few days back, forcing him out of town with nothing but the clothes on his back, taking his prized guns as a lesson.

"Say that again," Hayes said, his voice quieter now but no less menacing.

Alex gasped for air, his words tumbling out in a rush. "It was him, sheriff. He came back. I... I don't know where he went after, but he shot your deputies. They were just sitting at the table, and he walked in and gunned them down!"

Hayes let go of Alex and stepped back, pacing the length of the store. His mind was racing. That cowboy—he'd thought he'd broken him, sent him off humiliated, never to return. But the man had come back for revenge.

"And you didn't think to tell me this yesterday?" Hayes growled, glaring at Alex, who cowered against the wall.

"I—I was scared," Alex stammered. "Didn't want no part in it."

Hayes sneered. He didn't care about Alex's excuses. All that mattered now was finding that cowboy and putting him in the ground.

He stormed out of the store, his mind already made up. He couldn't do this alone. Not if that cowboy had friends with him. He needed more men who weren't afraid to get their hands dirty.

Which meant Pa Oakley.

The Oakley family had always been trouble, but they were the kind of trouble Hayes could use right now. If Hayes needed muscle, they were the men for the job. And the two men who were dead were Jed and Slade Oakley.

Hayes rode hard to the Oakley ranch, dust flying as his horse pounded the dry earth. When he arrived, Pa Oakley was sitting on the porch, chewing tobacco, his eyes narrowing as the sheriff approached. Pa Oakley was a hulking figure who wore his cruelty as plainly as the dust on his boots. His face was a roadmap of deep lines, etched by years of hard living and a harder heart, his eyes a steely, unforgiving grey that seemed to pierce right through a person's soul. His thin lips often pulled into a sneer, framed teeth yellowed by tobacco and neglect. A grizzled beard covered his jawline, speckled with grey.

He wore his clothes like armor—dust-caked jeans held up by a thick, cracked leather belt, with a battered hat casting a perpetual shadow over his face. His hands were like gnarled tree roots, calloused and rough, often clenched into fists that sent fear through those who crossed him. Pa Oakley was as mean as the desert sun and as unyielding as the rocks that dotted the land. No one ever mistook him for a kind man—his scowl alone was enough to drain the color from a man's face.

"What's this about, sheriff?" Pa Oakley drawled, though a glint in his eye betrayed that he already sensed trouble coming.

Sheriff Hayes didn't mince words. "Got bad news, Pa. Jed and Slade—they were gunned down at the saloon."

Pa Oakley shot to his feet, his face darkening, not with grief but with anger. "Somebody dared to shoot my boys?" He spat, more irked by the insult than the loss. "Who's fool enough to take on the Oakleys?"

A long silence settled between them as Pa Oakley's face twisted with rage, the veins in his neck straining. His hands clenched into fists, his breathing heavy, like a bull about to charge

Hayes nodded slowly. "We got cowboy trouble. Some half-breed injun cur I ran out of town came back and done for them. And I need your boys," Hayes said without preamble. "Got a man out there who needs killing. I want him found and dead by sundown."

Within minutes, Pa had rounded up Billy and Ted Oakley, their horses saddled and rifles strapped across their backs. They, too, were eager for blood.

The group rode back into town, Hayes leading them with a grim determination. As they galloped into the main street, the townsfolk scattered, ducking into doorways and windows. They knew this was going to get ugly. The Oakley boys had a reputation for solving problems with lead, and Hayes had brought them in to settle things the only way he knew how: with bullets.

Hayes nodded, his expression hard. "Word in town is that Alex Fisher, the storekeeper, saw it all godown. He's in the jail now."

Pa Oakley's eyes burned with fury, his jaw tight. "Bring me to him," he said, voice cold and final.

Pa Oakley's boots echoed on the wooden floor as he crossed the room, coming to stand before the cell. His eyes narrowed as he glared at Fisher. Behind him, Billy and Ted stood glowering at the man in the cell.

"So," Oakley sneered, his voice laced with venom, "you're tellin' folks it was an injun half-breed who did it. You bin protecting him?"

Fisher's chin lifted defiantly, but his hands trembled where he gripped the iron bars. "I had no part in what happened."

Pa Oakley's face twisted with rage, his eyes blazing. "You got a lot of nerve, Fisher. Reckon, it's time we teach you what happens when you cross an Oakley." He jerked his head at Hayes, his mouth set in a cruel line. "Open the cell."

Hayes didn't hesitate, drawing the key from his belt and unlocking the cell door. Fisher stumbled back, his eyes darting between the two men, panic creeping into his expression.

"Wait—you don't have to do this," he pleaded, desperation leaking into his voice. "I got a family—"

But Pa Oakley grabbed him by the collar, hauling him roughly from the cell, his face filled with a cold, merciless fury. Fisher struggled, but it was no use; Pa Oakley's grip was iron, and Hayes was there to shove him forward, forcing him toward the gallows tree outside the sheriff's office. Billy and Ted stood on either side of the tree, rifles ready, their eyes on the town.

As they dragged him from the sheriffs office to the gallows tree, the townsfolk began to emerge from hiding, drawn by the commotion. Their faces were pale, eyes wide with horror as they watched the two men lead Fisher to the tree, a long, gnarled branch stretching overhead like a skeletal arm. Pa Oakley pulled a rough rope from his saddlebag, tossing it to Hayes with a nod.

"Make it quick," he growled, his gaze fixed on Fisher, unblinking and remorseless.

Hayes looped the rope over the tree limb and fashioned a noose, slipping it around Fisher's neck as he pleaded, terror filling his voice. "Please, Pa, sheriff—don't do this. I'm beggin' ya."

But Oakley's face was stone, devoid of any mercy, his voice cold as death. "Beg all you want, Fisher. You turned your back on my family. And now you'll pay the price."

Hayes tightened the noose, stepping back to meet Oakley's gaze. Alex was standing on the ground; Pa took the loose end of the rope, mounted his horse, and wrapping the rope about the pommel, forced the animal forward, hauling Fisher from the ground towards the branch. Fisher's body jerked a dozen times, then stilled, the silence stretching over the town like a suffocating shroud. Pa released the rope, and the dead man fell in a heap to the ground.

Pa Oakley turned to face the townsfolk, his eyes burning with a deadly promise. "You all listen up!" he barked, his voice cutting through the air. "We'll hang another one of you every day until you find that injun cur, do you hear me? This is what happens when you cross an Oakley. Remember that."

Billy and Ted, whooping, fired their rifles towards the crowd, the townsfolk ran screaming for cover. Moments later, Hayes and the Oakleys mounted their horses, riding out of the street, leaving Fisher's body sprawled in a heap, a grim warning to all who watched.

CHAPTER FOURTEEN

.

The night wrapped around Nash like a worn blanket, quiet and endless save for the occasional pop and crackle from his campfire. He stretched out beside it, his saddle propped under his head, eyes fixed on the stars overhead. His horse shifted nearby, its injured leg still tender from their journey. Nash's mind drifted back to Buffalo Gap. But every time a memory started to surface, he forced it down, reminding himself he was done with that town and all its troubles.

When dawn broke, he rose, stamping out the dying embers of his fire before loading up his meagre belongings on his lame horse. It was slow going, his boots crunching over the dusty trail, one hand on the horse's reins as he led it carefully over the rough terrain. Somewhere on the horizon lay Abilene, and the promise of work and dollars that he badly needed.

Two days passed, and just as the early morning sun cast a pale light over the landscape, Nash heard it—the faint, steady beat of hooves pounding the ground. He tensed, hand drifting to the grip of his revolver, eyes scanning the trail. A lone rider tore across the plain, dust kicking up behind them like a rolling storm cloud. His eyes narrowed, and his hand tightened, poised to draw—until he recognized the rider.

Alice.

She reined in her horse, pulling up just short of him, her face flushed, her hair wild from the wind. Her eyes were wide and frantic, but as she dismounted, he noticed something else—a fierce determination.

"What are you doin' here, Alice?" he asked, crossing his arms and leveling her with a look.

She breathed in quickly, trying to steady herself. "Nash," she began, the words catching in her throat. "They're killing folks. Sheriff Hayes... he's back with the Oakley boys, and they're tearing Buffalo Gap apart to find you."

Nash's jaw tightened, his face darkening.

Alice's eyes dropped to the ground. "First thing they did was drag Alex Fisher out of his store... strung him up right in front of the sheriff's office. Sheriff Hayes called it 'a warning.' Said they'd hang another person every day until the town handed you over."

Nash felt a hollow, sinking feeling in his chest. He looked away, staring into the horizon as though he could put distance between himself and the anger rising inside him.

"They're terrorizing everyone, Nash," Alice said, her voice barely above a whisper. "Clem's rallying the town, saying they should just give you up to save themselves, send out men to bring you back. Only Callum's standing against them, but he can't hold them back forever."

Nash let out a bitter chuckle, shaking his head. "The folks of Buffalo Gap—too scared to stand up to a few brutes and a crooked sheriff. I should've known better."

113

Alice took a tentative step closer, her voice breaking through his brooding. "They're desperate, Nash. The Oakleys and Hayes... they'll burn that town to the ground if they have to."

He met her gaze, her blue eyes fixed on him with a mix of fear and determination. She was right, of course. The sherrif wasn't the type to let go of a grudge. But going back felt like walking into a trap. And this wasn't his fight!

"We don't have to go back, Alice," he said softly, the words almost painful. "You could come with me. We'd head to Abilene, start fresh."

Alice smiled faintly, though there was a sadness in it. "My family's back there, Nash. My pa, my sisters... I can't leave them to face the Oakleys alone. Running would be like abandoning them to the wolves."

Nash sighed, frustration creeping into his tone. "Alice, you've seen what they're willing to do. They'll bleed that whole town dry, and the folks there won't lift a finger to stop them."

Alice held his gaze, her voice steady but quiet. "Maybe. But Buffalo Gap's all I've ever known. Those people—they're my kin. And if I have to fight for them or run... well, I think you know what I'd choose."

Nash watched her, admiration mingling with irritation. He wanted to shake some sense into her, but he knew better than to try. "You're braver than most, I'll give you that," he muttered. "Braver than me, probably."

Alice laughed softly, and the sound was like a balm on the tense morning air. "I don't know about that. But I've made my choice. I'll stand by those folks."

Nash grunted, his face hardening with resolve. "Then I'll go back with you. Someone's gotta stand by you, and I don't see any of the men in Buffalo Gap lining up to volunteer."

Alice looked up, surprise and relief flickering in her eyes. "What's the plan, then?"

"I've not figured that part out yet," he replied, his mouth curling into a smirk. "First, we've got to get there." He nodded toward her horse. "The only way we'll make it is by riding double, and we'll have to go slow to spare my buckskin's leg."

Alice nodded, understanding. "She'll make it as long as we take it easy."

They spent the next few minutes arranging his gear, saddling her horse and leading his alongside. Nash checked the reins, cinching them tight, his movements methodical. He didn't much like the idea of putting Alice in danger, but there was no other way.

"All right, get up first," he said, gesturing to the saddle.

Alice mounted, shifting to make room as Nash climbed up behind her. The horse huffed, adjusting to the extra weight, and Nash kept a steady hold on his buckskin's reins as they set off

They rode in silence for a while, the horse's slow, steady gait lulling them into an uneasy quiet. The air was heavy and thick with the smell of dust and impending heat.

Every now and then, Alice glanced over her shoulder at him, her expression torn between worry and resolve.

"You know, Nash, you don't have to do this," she murmured after a while. "They're just as likely to turn on you as they are to help."

Nash shrugged, his gaze fixed on the trail ahead. "Maybe. But I can't leave you to face those killers alone."

She fell silent, but he felt the weight of her gratitude in the gentle way she leaned back against him, and he enjoyed feeling her close to him.

"Thank you," she said after a time, her voice barely audible over the steady crunch of hooves on the trail.

"For what?" Nash asked, glancing down at her.

"For going back with me," she replied softly. "Even though you don't owe them a thing. I know it's not easy."

Nash let out a rueful laugh. "Easy? No, ma'am, I wouldn't say that. But it's the right thing to do. And I reckon that's what counts."

Alice gave a soft laugh. After a while, they lapsed into silence again, each of them lost in thought.

Every mile closer to Buffalo Gap felt like a step into the jaws of a trap, but Nash kept his face stony, his gaze fixed on the road. He'd made his decision, and if the town would have him as a sacrifice, well, he'd make them work for it. One thing was for sure. He wasn't letting Alice go back alone.

After a few hours, Alice spoke up, breaking the silence with an unexpected question. "You think they'll let us walk right in, or are they likely to throw us a welcome party?"

Nash's mouth quirked up in a grin. "Oh, I reckon Sheriff Hayes will have his red carpet rolled out for me. Just picture it—a noose, a few deputies, maybe a couple of Oakleys waiting to shake my hand."

She snorted. "Sounds like a real royal affair."

"Only the best for Buffalo Gap's most wanted," Nash replied, his voice dripping with sarcasm.

They shared a quiet laugh, a moment of levity that seemed to lighten the burden between them. For a few moments, the tension eased, and they rode together in companionable silence, the weight of what awaited them held at bay.

The sun dipped in the sky, casting long shadows across the land, and Nash caught sight of Buffalo Gap on the horizon. The town looked small and quiet, nestled under the vast expanse of the sky like a predator lying in wait.

Alice turned her head to him, her gaze steady. "Ready?"

Nash nodded, a grim smile playing on his lips. "As I'll ever be."

They nudged the horse forward, and the town drew closer, each step carrying them back into the heart of danger.

CHAPTER FIFTEEN

The afternoon sun burned low over Buffalo Gap as Sheriff Hayes and the Oakley boys rode back into town, dust rising in clouds around their horses. The townsfolk watched from behind closed doors and shaded windows, faces pale, eyes full of fear as the men moved up the main street. Hayes's face was set in a dark scowl, and beside him, Pa Oakley's eyes gleamed with a cold, murderous intent.

They reined their horses to a stop outside the sheriff's office, and Hayes swung down, his boots hitting the ground with a heavy thud. He scanned the silent street, his hand resting on the revolver at his side. The Oakley boys dismounted, each armed and eager, their faces twisted with the same ruthless anger that marked their father's gaze.

"Alright!" Hayes's voice bellowed, breaking the quiet. "Listen up, Buffalo Gap!" He took a step forward, eyes sweeping over the faces peering from windows, lurking in shadows. "We're here for the half-breed! And we ain't leavin' until he's brought to us. I know damn well he was here, and somebody in this town knows where he went."

Silence met his words, a thick, suffocating quiet as no one dared step forward. The townsfolk shifted, casting anxious glances at one another, fear etched into every face. Hayes's scowl deepened, and he drew his pistol, his eyes settling on the saloon across the street.

He strode forward, his boots kicking up puffs of dust with each step, until he reached the saloon's double doors and flung them open. His gaze locked onto Callum, who was wiping down the bar, his face a mask of forced calm.

"Callum, you know where that halbreed went?" Hayes sneered, his voice low and filled with menace. "Get out here." He jerked his head toward the street, and behind him, Pa Oakley and his boys waited, their hands on their guns, their expressions promising nothing but violence.

Callum straightened, his jaw clenched, a flicker of defiance in his eyes, though he kept his tone respectful. "Sheriff, I don't know where he went," he said, his voice even. "He left town days ago."

Hayes's eyes narrowed, his expression cold. "See, that's a problem, Callum, 'cause your saloon was the last place that injun cur was seen. And you can bet that don't sit right with me. Or with Pa Oakley."

Pa Oakley stepped forward, his face twisted in rage. "My boys, Jed and Slade—they died in that saloon of yours, Callum," he growled. "You let that snake in, let him gun 'em down."

Callum met his gaze, his hands steady though he was surrounded by deadly eyes. "Nash didn't come lookin' for trouble, Oakley," he said, his voice low but firm. "Your boys were the ones who drew first."

Pa Oakley's face twisted further, his anger bubbling over. "You got a lot of nerve, Callum, talkin' to me about my boys. You let Nash kill 'em right under your nose, and you expect to get away with it?" He turned to the crowd gathering in the street, his voice booming. "This man is just as guilty—he harbored a killer."

Hayes nodded, the cold smile on his face spreading as he raised his pistol, pointing it at Callum's chest. "If the injun ain't here to answer for himself, then you'll be the one to pay for what happened."

The townsfolk murmured in fear, but none stepped forward to intervene, Pa Oakley's glare kept them rooted in place. Callum glanced around at his neighbors, his face resigned but unyielding.

"Do what you will, Sheriff," Callum said quietly, his voice strong. "I may not have fought back then, but I'll sure as hell die standing now."

Hayes cocked the gun, the metallic click echoing across the street, but before he could pull the trigger, Pa Oakley strode forward, his own gun raised. His face was contorted with fury and rage.

"Step aside, Hayes," Oakley spat, his voice low and seething. "I'll take care of this myself."

Callum looked at Pa Oakley with pity and defiance in his eyes, but he held his ground. Oakley sneered, lifting the gun, his finger tightening on the trigger. Without a word, he fired. The shot rang out, cracking the air, and Callum staggered back, a dark stain blooming across his chest as he sank to his knees, his expression still fierce even as he fell.

The townsfolk gasped, some of them crying out, others frozen in shock, watching helplessly as Callum's body slumped into the dust, his blood soaking into the dirt of the street.

Pa Oakley turned, his gaze cold as steel as he surveyed the crowd. "This is what happens when you cross an Oakley!" he roared. "Every last one of you is responsible for what happened to my boys. And I'll make damn sure you pay."

Hayes stepped forward, his own expression hard. "We'll be back here tomorrow," he announced, his voice carrying over the terrified crowd. "And if that injun ain't here by then, one of you will take his place." He looked around, letting his words sink in, watching the fear spread across the faces before him.

With that, Pa Oakley and his sons turned, mounting their horses, Hayes at their side. They rode out of town, leaving a trail of dust and silence in their wake. The townsfolk watched, their faces pale, as Callum's body lay still in the street, a dark reminder of the price Buffalo Gap would pay if Nash didn't return.

And as the dust settled, the people of Buffalo Gap knew that their time was running out.

The night air was thick and silent as Nash and Alice rode up to the outskirts of Buffalo Gap, the distant shapes of the buildings barely visible in the dark. They reined their horses to a stop, dismounting quietly and tethering them in the brush, hidden from the street. Nash turned to Alice, his gaze steady but firm.

"Let's get you home," he said softly. "Town doesn't need any more reasons to turn on your family."

Alice nodded, her face pale in the dim moonlight, but her eyes were determined. She followed Nash as he led the way through back alleys and shadowed paths, every step bringing them closer to the heart of Buffalo Gap. When they reached her father's house, they paused in the shadows, and Nash took her hand, his grip warm and solid.

"Stay inside, Alice," he murmured, his voice low but filled with quiet authority. "There's nothin' you can do now that won't get you hurt."

Alice met his gaze, her voice trembling but firm. "Promise me, Nash," she whispered, eyes shining. "Promise me you'll make them pay for what they've done."

Nash gave a curt nod, his jaw set. "I intend to."

He watched her disappear into the house, waiting until the door closed behind her before turning back to the street, his eyes hard as steel as he headed for the barn. Moving with quiet precision, he slipped inside, his steps soft on the hay-strewn floor. In the faint light, he pulled his gun from its holster, checking each piece with a practiced hand. When he left Bufalo Gap he had every intention of earing his own gun belt and having both his Colts and the old Perry one shot back in his possession.

As he slid fresh rounds into his revolver, he heard faint footsteps behind him and looked up to see Hank, eyes wide and filled with a mixture of fear and grief.

"Alice told me you were here. They killed Callum, Nash," Hank whispered, his voice was choked with emotion. "Shot him down like a dog. Said he was responsible for what happened to Jed and Slade."

Nash's face darkened, his expression hardening into a mask of fury. He knew the Oakleys had no conscience, but Callum... Callum had been a good man, the only one willing to stand up for what was right. Nash's hands clenched, the cold metal of the revolver pressing against his skin as his anger boiled over, fierce and deadly.

"Rest of the town's scared outta their minds," Hank continued, voice shaking. "Sheriff Hayes said they'll hang another one tomorrow if we don't hand you over."

Nash said nothing, his eyes fixed on the Colt as he snapped the chamber shut. But inside, he felt a burning determination, the kind that only came from knowing he had nothing left to lose.

"They won't have the chance," he muttered, slipping the revolver back into its holster. He reached for his rifle, checking the barrel, the sights, every piece as if his life depended on it. Because, come morning, it just might.

Hank hesitated, glancing nervously toward the door. "What're you gonna do, Nash?"

Nash's eyes narrowed, a grim smile tugging at the corner of his mouth. "I'm gonna be waiting," he replied, his voice low and filled with cold resolve. "When they ride back in, they'll find me ready."

Hank nodded, his face a mixture of awe and dread as he slipped out of the barn, leaving Nash alone once more. In the silence, Nash stood there, his heart steady, his gaze fixed on Bufalo Gap beyond the open barn door as he waited for the first light of dawn to break. When the sheriff and the Oakleys came looking for blood, he'd be there, ready to meet them.

Ready to end it.

CHAPTER SIXTEEN

The sun was barely up as Sheriff Hayes and the Oakleys rode back into town. Dust swirled around them as they pulled their horses to a halt in the center of the main street, their figures dark against the early morning light. Pa Oakley dismounted first, his face twisted with fury, his hand resting on the butt of his gun, ready to draw. Beside him, his sons, each a spitting image of their father's rage, sat on their horses, scowling at the empty street.

Sheriff Hayes stepped forward, casting a contemptuous glare at the closed doors and drawn curtains that lined the street. He raised his voice, letting it boom through the quiet, empty town.

"Alright, Buffalo Gap!" Hayes bellowed, his voice sharp and cold. "No more games. You got one chance to save your skins." He paused, giving the doors and windows a long, hard look. "Bring out the half-breed, right here in the street, and no one else has to get hurt!"

But the only answer was silence, thick and heavy, as the townsfolk hid behind their walls, huddled in fear. Hayes mouth twisted in a sneer, his hand drifting toward his pistol as he exchanged a glance with Pa Oakley

Pa Oakley stepped forward, his voice a low growl. "You heard the sheriff!" he shouted, his voice dripping with fury. "So here's how this is gonna go—either you bring him out, or someone else pays the price."

Still, no one moved. Curtains fluttered as unseen eyes watched from the shadows, but no one dared speak, no one dared face the men in the street. Pa Oakley's patience thinned, his face growing darker as he scanned the silent buildings, his eyes narrowing in a mix of anger and disgust.

"Fine," Hayes spat, his tone laced with menace. "You're makin' this harder than it needs to be. So we'll start takin' folks out one by one. Let's see if that rattles any sense into you."

"Bring some of the women out into the street. We'll see how long it takes for someone to talk once we start putting guns to their heads," Hayes said to Billy and Ted, his voice booming through the silent town.

Pa Oakley grinned, and his sons followed suit, eyes gleaming with a dangerous hunger. Billy Oakley was the first to move, stalking up to one of the houses. The door was barely latched before he kicked it open, stepping inside with his rifle slung lazily over his shoulder.

"Come on out, ladies," Billy drawled, his voice sickeningly sweet. Moments later, a woman's scream cut through the silence. It didn't take long before they dragged out three women, forcing them into the street.

Among them was Alice, her pale blue dress dusty from the dirt, her hair disheveled from the rough handling of Billy Oakley, who held her by the arm. Her eyes darted around, wide with fear but still holding defiance as she was pulled into the center of town, where Hayes stood waiting.

Hayes stepped closer, his gaze sweeping over the women. He knew Alice—knew she was Hank's daughter, one of the few with enough spirit left to talk back. He stepped toward her, a cruel smirk tugging at his lips.

"Alice," Hayes said, his voice low and menacing. "You know where he is, don't you? You tell me, and we'll let you go. Otherwise..." He glanced toward Ted Oakley, who was grinning like a devil. "Well, you don't want to know otherwise."

Alice lifted her chin, trying to keep her voice steady, though her heart was pounding in her chest. "I don't know where Nash is. He left days ago," she said, meeting Hayes' gaze with as much courage as she could muster. "And even if I did, I wouldn't tell you."

Hayes' smile faded. "Wrong answer." Hayes's hand wrapped around her arm, and he dragged her close to him, the cold steel of his piece pressing against her temple. A man rushed out of the livery, running as fast as his old legs could carry him. Hank, Alice's father, his face etched with desperation, came stumbling into the scene, gasping for breath.

"Leave her alone, Hayes!" Hank shouted, stumbling toward them. "She doesn't know nothin'! You don't have to do this!"

But Hayes barely glanced at Hank, his cold eyes fixed on Alice. "If you won't talk, someone else will. Ain't that right, Hank?"

Hank's chest heaved, his eyes darting to Alice, then back to the sheriff. He hesitated for a heartbeat before he blurted out, "Nash... Nash is in the livery yard."

The street went dead silent.

In the barn, Nash heard it too, Hank's panicked voice rang in his ears.

"Damn it, Hank," Nash muttered under his breath, his hands gripping the Colt. He knew what was coming. He'd wanted to make his move on his own terms, but he didn't suppose it mattered.

Outside, Hayes' lips curled into a cruel smile. "Go flush him out. Shoot him if you see him."

Nash peered through a crack in the barn doors, seeing Ted and Billy Oakley already mounting up, rifles at the ready. They were coming for him. He clenched his jaw, feeling the weight of the decision pressing down on him. His eyes narrowed as he looked out at the Oakleys preparing to ride toward the barn and then to Alice, who stood trembling in the street, her father beside her.

Nash let out a long, slow breath. He knew what he had to do.

As the Oakleys started toward the livery, Nash stepped out of the shadows, gun in his hand. He moved quickly, stepping into the barn's wide-open doorway. His silhouette was stark against the afternoon sun, and Billy Oakley spotted him the second he showed himself.

"There he is!" Billy shouted.

"This is between you and me, sherrif!" Nash shouted back, his voice booming across the dusty street. He stepped forward into the street; his piece was in the holster. It was a gamble – a big gamble. Would the Oakley boys fire, or would they wait and relish watching the spectacle of a standoff between Hayes and Nash? "You want me? Here I am."

The Oakleys reined in their horses, eyes fixed on Nash as he stepped further into the open. Pa Oakley sneered, already reaching for his gun. But Nash wasn't looking at him—he was looking at Sheriff Hayes.

"Let Alice go," Nash called out, his voice hard as steel.

Hayes pushed Alice away from him and sauntered forward, his eyes cold and sharp as a rattlesnake's. "You're damn right it is," he spat. "You gunned down my deputies, *suuun.* This is justice."

Nash's jaw tightened.

For a moment, everything stood still, the air heavy with the threat of violence. Nash's fingers itched near the trigger, and he could feel every eye in town on him. There would be no backing down now.

Then, Sheriff Hayes smiled—a slow, dangerous smile. "You're right about one thing, *suuun,*" he said. "This is between us. But it won't end with you. After you're dead, I'll finish what I started."

Nash glanced at Alice, her face pale but her eyes fierce and worried. He nodded once, almost imperceptibly, and then turned his full attention back to Hayes.

"Let's settle it then," Nash said, his voice low and deadly. "Right here. Right now."

The street fell silent as the two men squared off, the whole town holding its breath for the gunfight that was about to erupt as Nash and Sheriff Hayes faced each other. The early morning sun cast shadows across the worn ground. The air between them was thick with tension as if the town was bracing for the storm of violence about to explode.

Nash stood steady, feet planted firmly in the dirt, his hands hovering near the grip of his Colt. His guns had been taken from him by Hayes—stolen, like so many other things the sheriff had taken in his time. But now, at least one of them was back in Nash's hands, and there was a certain justice in that. His eyes narrowed, locking onto Hayes, reading every movement, every breath. He knew this moment had been coming ever since he'd walked into this godforsaken town.

Across from him, Sheriff Hayes stood with his feet set wide, his gun holstered but his fingers flexing at his side. His face was a mask of arrogance and anticipation. He was sure of his skill and had nothing to judge the other man by. As far as Hayes was concerned, this would be an easy kill—one that would be witnessed by the townsfolk tightening the hold he had over them, choking them with fear.

The wind kicked up a bit of dust between them, and in the distance, the soft whinny of a horse cut through the tense silence. The Oakley boys watched from their horses. Alice stood frozen with the other women on the other side of the street, her eyes locked on Nash, silently willing him to survive this. Her father, Hank, hovered beside her, helpless but desperate, knowing that a wrong move could cost them everything.

The street was deathly quiet. The only sounds were the steady breathing of two men, each waiting for the other to make the first move. Nash had patience, endless patience.

Time stretched thin, a single heartbeat lasting forever.

And then it happened.

A flash of movement caught Nash's eye.

Hayes' fingers twitch toward the gun at his hip.

Time seemed to slow. Every nerve in Nash's body reacted with honed instinct, his senses heightened, his focus narrowing to a single point. There was no room for hesitation; he'd seen men die for less. The glint of sunlight on Hayes revolver flashed like a signal fire, and in that fraction of a heartbeat, Nash knew it was him or Hayes.

In a blur, Nash's right hand dropped to his own revolver, his fingers curling around the grip with a familiarity that felt as natural as breathing. The smooth wood felt warm and solid. It felt like his hand and the gun were one, an extension of his own will.

Before Hayes could finish drawing his gun, Nash had his revolver halfway clear of the holster. The world around him faded—no more shouting townsfolk, no clinking spurs or creaking leather—only the steady, calm rhythm of his own breath and the cold steel in his hand.

The barrel cleared the leather, and as it did, his body moved instinctively, a fluid shift of weight that brought his entire frame into perfect alignment. His finger found the trigger just as the sights met his line of vision, centering on Hayes's chest, a target painted clear as day. Without so much as a second thought, Nash pulled the trigger, feeling the gun kick back in his hand as a single, sharp explosion echoed through the dusty street.

The bullet struck true, catching Hayes in the shoulder and spinning him sideways, his gun clattering to the ground as his body twisted with the force of the shot. He staggered back, a look of shock flickering across his face before it hardened into one of fury. Blood seeped through his shirt, spreading in a dark stain as he clutched at his wound, struggling to stay on his feet. But Nash didn't lower his gun. He stood motionless, the smoke curling from the barrel of the Colt as he kept his aim steady, ready for any hint of movement.

The silence that followed was absolute, a thick, tense quiet that seemed to stretch on forever. The townsfolk, who had been watching from the safety of their windows and doorways, held their breath, caught between awe and terror as they watched Hayes stumble, his face twisted in pain and rage.

Slowly, Hayes' eyes lifted to meet Nash's, burning with hatred and disbelief. His hand trembled as it hovered over his injured shoulder, but he made no move to reach for his fallen weapon. Instead, he glared at Nash with a look that promised retribution, the weight of every threat he'd ever made clear in that moment.

But Nash's gaze was cold and unyielding, his finger still resting on the trigger, ready to fire again if Hayes so much as blinked the wrong way. He took a slow step forward, his boots crunching in the dust, his voice low and steady.

"Go on, Hayes," he said, his tone edged with ice. "Try it again if you're feelin' lucky."

The challenge hung in the air, sharp as the gunpowder still lingering in the breeze. For a moment, it seemed like Hayes might take the bait, his jaw tightening as his fingers twitched, his pride pushing him to the edge. But then his gaze flickered to the revolver on the ground, not far away but as good as a mile in that instant.

In a final act of defiance, Hayes sneered, spitting blood-tinged saliva onto the ground at Nash's feet. "This ain't over, Nash," he ground out, his voice laced with venom. "Not by a damn sight."

But Nash's face didn't change. He simply tightened his grip on the revolver, his stare as unyielding as granite. "Maybe not, sheriff. But for now, it looks like you're done."

With that, Nash took a step back, lowering his gun just slightly enough to let Hayes know the encounter was over—for the moment. The sheriff, still clutching his bleeding shoulder, turned, stumbling as he made his way back toward the line of Oakley men who had been watching, frozen, from the other side of the street. None of them moved to help him.

Nash held his ground, his revolver still in his hand, and watched as Sheriff Hayes staggered toward his horse, each step labored and heavy. The man clutched his bleeding shoulder, a hand pressed against the wound that still seeped dark, sticky blood. Dust rose around him, mingling with the faint tendrils of smoke that drifted from the barrel of Nash's

Colt, still gripped firmly in his hand. The silence was thick, punctuated only by the sheriff's uneven footsteps.

Reaching his horse, Hayes leaned against the saddle, his forehead pressed hard against the worn leather, his breaths coming in shallow, painful gasps. He looked beaten, shoulders hunched, and for a brief moment, Nash wondered if that was the end of it. Maybe Hayes would accept his fate, mount up, and ride out, his pride wounded as much as his body. But then Nash saw it—a subtle shift in Hayes' stance, a steeling of resolve that sent a prickle of unease through him.

Nash's grip tightened instinctively on the Colt as he studied Hayes, who seemed to be gathering himself, muttering something low and guttural under his breath. Hayes straightened slightly, his hand sliding down along the saddle in a practiced motion. In one smooth, swift movement, Hayes reached across the saddle, his fingers closing around the stock of the rifle that was mounted in the saddle holster.

Nash saw the glint of the metal an instant before Hayes whipped around, the sheriff's face twisted in a mix of desperation and pure rage. The rifle swung up, the barrel aimed squarely at Nash, and Hayes's finger tightened on the trigger, the barrel barely aligned.

Nash was already moving. In a blur, he raised the Colt, his hand steady, his eyes focused. Time slowed, the tension thickening as he zeroed in on Hayes, everything else falling away. Just as Hayes's rifle sighted on him, Nash's Colt barked out a second time.

The shot cracked through the still morning, shattering the quiet like a thunderclap. The bullet struck Hayes square in the chest, the impact knocking him backwards as though an invisible force had yanked him off his feet. His rifle slipped from his grasp, clattering to the ground, his fingers loosening their grip as his body crumpled.

For a brief, suspended moment, Hayes's eyes were wide, a flicker of stunned realization dancing in their depths before they dulled. He collapsed against his horse, his legs giving way as he sank heavily to the ground, dust billowing around him. His hat tumbled off, landing in the dirt beside him as his body fell still, lifeless, sprawled at the feet of his horse.

Nash kept his gun trained on the sheriff's motionless form, every muscle tense. His gaze locked on Hayes' face, searching for any sign of movement. But there was nothing—only the eerie stillness that follows a violent end. The townsfolk, who had been watching from windows and doorways, held their collective breath, the weight of what they had witnessed sinking in like lead.

CHAPTER SEVENTEEN

Hayes lay sprawled in the dirt, his lifeless eyes staring up at the vast, unforgiving sky, blood pooling around him. The townsfolk watched from their hiding places, horror etched on every face as they realized the sheriff was gone and the worst was yet to come.

Pa Oakley stood frozen for a second, his face twisted in disbelief and fury, before he turned to his sons, his voice bellowing out into the chaos.

"Gun him down, boys!" he roared, his snarling command echoing through the empty street.

Without hesitation, the Oakley boys raised their rifles, firing in a furious volley as Nash dove to the side, his own gun blazing. He got off four quick shots, seeing one of the Oakleys stagger as his bullet found its mark, but then his revolver clicked, empty.

Nash hit the ground hard, rolling behind a water trough as bullets splintered the wood around him, sending splashes of muddy water into the air. The crack of gunfire echoed down the street, and he could hear the panicked screams of townsfolk running for cover, doors slamming shut, windows shattering as people scrambled to escape the line of fire. Dust and smoke filled the air, choking and thick, as the Oakleys continued firing, their anger spurring them on, their shouts cutting through the haze.

"Come out and die, injun!" one of the Oakley boys snarled, his voice filled with rage.

Pa Oakley's voice rose above the din, seething and furious. "You killed my boys. This town ain't big enough to hide you!"

Nash's hands moved swiftly, his heart pounding as he reloaded his revolver with practiced efficiency, each round clicking into place as he counted them. He could hear Pa Oakley pacing in the street, his boots crunching over the dirt, each step heavy with a threat.

"We'll drag you out of there, Nash!" Oakley yelled, his voice dripping with menace. "You don't stand a chance. There's nowhere left to run."

Nash closed the chamber on his gun, his hand steady, his gaze hard. He glanced over the edge of the water trough, catching sight of Pa Oakley and his remaining son at his side in the street, pistols at the ready, their eyes scanning for any sign of movement. He knew they'd be waiting for him to make a move, just itching for a clean shot.

From inside one of the nearby buildings, he caught a flicker of movement—a frightened face peering out from behind a half-closed door, townsfolk caught between their fear and their guilt, watching helplessly as the standoff unfolded before them. Nash's mouth set into a grim line.

This was it.

Pa Oakley's voice rang out again, sharp and taunting. "You're alone, Nash. No one's comin' to help you. The only thing waitin' for you out here is a bullet."

Nash tightened his grip on the revolver, feeling the familiar weight steady him. He took a deep breath, forcing aside the ache in his shoulder from his rough landing, and gauged the distance between him and the Oakleys. The water trough wouldn't provide cover for much longer—they'd either close in on him or flush him out. He needed a plan, and he needed it fast.

He glanced around, taking stock of the scene: the livery just to his right, a stack of barrels by the saloon steps, and a broken wagon wheel lying in the dust near the far side of the street. It wasn't much, but he could make it work. He shifted his weight, preparing himself, feeling the adrenaline surge as he steeled himself for what came next.

With a sharp inhale, Nash sprang up, firing a quick shot in Pa Oakley's direction, then darted to the side, making a break for the barrels. The Oakley boy fired, bullets whizzing past Nash as he moved, his boots pounding against the dirt. He dove behind the barrels, breathless but unharmed, his heart pounding as he heard Pa Oakley curse, reloading in frustration.

"You ain't getting away, half-breed!" the younger Oakley snarled, his voice tight with fury. "Face us like a man!"

Nash kept low, his mind racing. He knew he had only seconds before they'd pin him down again. He took a steadying breath, his grip tightening on the revolver. He knew how this would end, knew he was outnumbered and outgunned, but there was

138

no backing down now. He'd come here to face them, and he'd see it through.

Nash gritted his teeth, anger boiling in his veins. He took a quick glance around, mapping out his next move. The Oakleys were circling, closing in, their faces twisted with fury, their guns aimed and ready. The showdown was coming, fast and fierce. With one last steadying breath, he prepared himself to face whatever came next. He was a lone man against the Oakleys, but he'd make sure they remembered him.

Nash dashed from behind the barrels, his heart pounding as he sprinted toward the cover of the saloon. Bullets whizzed past him, splintering wood and kicking up dust, the Oakleys shouting as they aimed. He bounded up the steps two at a time, his boots echoing on the wooden boards, and pushed through the batwing doors, diving for cover as he entered the dim, shadowed interior.

The glass shattered behind him as bullets ripped through the windows, shards raining down onto the worn wooden floor. Nash stayed low, taking a breath as he felt the solid wall of the saloon against his back, the familiar scent of stale whiskey and dry wood around him. Outside, the Oakleys were still yelling, their taunts punctuated by the sporadic crack of gunfire.

"Think you can hide in there forever?" Billy shouted, his voice filled with fury. "We'll burn that saloon to the ground if we have to!"

Nash's jaw tightened, but before he could respond, he heard a soft rustle nearby. He turned to see Marthe, the saloon owner's widow, standing a few feet away, her husband's old rifle clutched tightly in her hands. Her face was drawn, her eyes fierce, but there was a spark of determination there that hadn't dimmed, even in the face of the Oakleys' wrath.

"Didn't expect to see you here, Nash," Marthe whispered, her voice steady despite the chaos around them. "But if you're here to end this, I've got your back."

Nash gave her a grim nod, respect in his eyes. "Didn't mean to drag you into this, ma'am," he said, glancing toward the shattered windows. "But they're not giving us much choice."

Marthe's mouth twisted into a wry smile, her grip tightening on the rifle. "No choice but to fight back, then."

She glanced toward the door, her eyes sharp, calculating. "I'll stay here, let them think you're still holed up. You slip out the back and circle around behind them." Her gaze flicked back to him, a hint of steel in her expression. "They'll be too busy firing on me to notice you."

Nash grinned, a fierce spark lighting his eyes. "I hope you're a good shot, Marthe?"

"Good enough," she replied, a determined set to her jaw. "Now, go. Don't keep me waiting. I've only got three rounds left."

Nash hesitated. Then in a quick move he unhooked the Henry from his back and put it on the table next to Marthe. "You got another fifteen now."

140

Marthe nodded. "I'll make them count. Now go."

Nash nodded, giving her a final look of respect, then turned and slipped through the saloon's back door. Hoping that she could buy him enough time to get where he needed to be before they realized she was out of bullets. The alleyway was dark, shielded from the main street by the buildings on either side, giving him the cover he needed. He kept low, making his way along the narrow path as he listened to the gunfire echoing from the saloon, each shot a distraction pulling the Oakleys' attention.

Inside, Marthe took up a position by the shattered window, a box of cartridges next to her, aiming her husband's rifle toward the street. She fired a shot, her aim steady, the rifle's report cutting through the Oakleys' taunts. She could hear them cursing, see their angry faces as they ducked for cover, the realization slowly dawning on them that this fight wasn't going to be as easy as they'd hoped.

"You got nowhere to go!" Pa Oakley bellowed, his voice dripping with rage. "We'll tear that place apart if we have to!"

Marthe fired again, the shot going wide but enough to keep the Oakleys pinned down, their attention focused on the saloon's front. She could feel her pulse racing, but she held her ground, buying Nash the precious moments he needed to get into position.

The rifle clicked – empty. She abandoned it and picked up the Henry.

Outside, Nash moved swiftly, circling around to the far side of the street, keeping low as he crept closer to the Oakleys' position. He spotted the two of them huddled behind the cover of a stack of crates, their attention fixed on the saloon. Pa Oakley was shouting orders, directing his son to keep firing, their guns aimed relentlessly at the saloon's front.

Nash took a deep breath, his revolver loaded, his rifle at the ready. He knew he only had one shot at this, one chance to catch them off guard before they realized he wasn't inside the saloon. His gaze hardened as he steadied himself, his grip firm, his resolve set. He moved out from the shadows with a quick, silent step, raising his Colt and taking aim.

CHAPTER EIGHTEEN

Nash crept forward, staying low as he moved into range, his breath steady, the Colt raised. Pa Oakley and his son were crouched behind the pile of crates Nash had sheltered behind earlier, their backs to him, still firing on the saloon, completely unaware that the tables had turned. He was running low on ammunition—just a few rounds left in his revolver.

He knew he had to make every one of them count. Steadying his aim, he exhaled slowly. Pa Oakley was his target. But a sharp voice broke the silence just as he was about to squeeze the trigger.

"Pa! He's behind you!" Nash's gaze darted to the Oakley boy he'd wounded earlier, who was slumped against a wall, blood darkening his shoulder, his eyes wide with alarm.

Nash didn't have a moment to waste—he fired, his shot close enough to send Pa Oakley's hat flying but not close enough to do any real damage. As they spotted him, Oakley and his son whirled around, their faces twisted in fury.

"Get him!" Pa Oakley shouted, his voice filled with rage, and the Oakleys opened fire.

Bullets whizzed past Nash as he ducked and darted for cover. He sprinted across the street, his boots kicking up dust as he dashed for the closest building—the broken-down storefront of Alex Fisher's general store. He threw himself through the doorway, feeling the rush of cool, stale air inside the dim interior. Cans and boxes scattered across the floor, Nash waded through the clutter, his boots slipping on a few cans as he moved deeper into the store, his eyes scanning for an exit at the back. Outside, he could hear Pa Oakley and his son regrouping, their boots pounding against the dirt as they advanced, shouting to one another as they surrounded the store. Nash's mind raced as he stepped around a fallen shelf, moving carefully to avoid knocking anything over. He could feel the weight of his limited ammunition, the few rounds he had left barely enough for one last stand.

His eyes flickered over the shelves, searching desperately, and then his gaze landed on a dusty box, nearly hidden behind a row of canned goods. He grabbed it, his heart racing as he tore it open, revealing a stash of cartridges—enough to buy him a fighting chance. Nash loaded his Colt with quick, practiced hands, feeling the cold weight of the bullets settle into the chamber. He took a deep breath, steadying himself as he slid the rest of the cartridges into his pocket, his mind racing through his options.

The back of the store led to a narrow alley, an escape route that would give him cover. But Pa Oakley wouldn't stay put for long, and once they realized he was on the move, the chase would only grow fiercer.

Outside, Pa Oakley's voice rang out, laced with fury. "You can't hide forever!" he shouted, his tone filled with menace. "We're comin' in there, and when we find you, there'll be hell to pay!"

Nash's jaw clenched, his resolve hardening as he took one last look at the interior of the store. He'd have to be smart, every shot precise, every move calculated. The Oakleys were closing in, and he knew that his next step could make the difference between life and death. With a final glance around, he moved toward the back, weaving through the mess of spilled goods and broken shelves, his newly-loaded Colt clutched tightly in his hand. He could hear the Oakleys just outside the door, their footsteps heavy, their voices taunting. But Nash wasn't done yet. As he slipped toward the back exit, he steeled himself, ready to take the fight to them on his terms.

Nash pressed himself tight against the side of the building, his breath shallow as he listened to the rapid gunfire shredding the wooden walls around him. Splinters and dust flew through the air, each bullet chipping away at the old structure, the Oakleys firing blindly from behind the general store. He knew he couldn't stay hidden for long, but he waited, counting the seconds, listening intently for any sign of an advantage.

And then, there it was—the unmistakable click of a gun hitting an empty chamber.

Nash's instincts kicked in, his hand tightening around the grip of his Colt. He knew he had a split second, a narrow window before they reloaded or moved. His muscles coiled, and with one fluid motion, he rounded the corner, gun raised, his gaze zeroing in on the two figures.

There was Billy, his face flushed with frustration, fumbling to reload, his hands shaking as he struggled to slap more bullets into his revolver. His eyes went wide with shock as he saw Nash emerge, his gun still aimed but useless, the chamber empty.

Billy Oakley's hand twitched, his gaze darting nervously between Nash and his father. For a moment, it looked as though he would drop his gun. But in a flash, his eyes hardened, and instead, he whirled and dove back through the back door of the store.

"Damn it," Nash muttered under his breath, his focus flickering to the doorway. That brief second of distraction was all Pa Oakley needed. With a sudden burst of desperate energy, Pa lunged at Nash, tackling him hard, and they both went down in a swirl of dust and fury. Nash hit the ground with a bone-jarring thud, his Colt slipping from his hand as they rolled across the gritty earth.

Pa Oakley's hands were rough and relentless, fingers clawing for any hold he could get. He drove his knee into Nash's ribs, a sneer of triumph twisting his face. "You ain't takin' down my family," he spat, his voice a low, venomous growl.

Nash gritted his teeth, throwing a sharp elbow into Pa's side, forcing him to loosen his grip just enough for Nash to twist free. They scrambled in the dirt, kicking up dust and grappling with raw, unfiltered rage. Nash's fingers stretched toward his gun, just

146

out of reach, but Pa Oakley tackled him again, forcing him down, his weight pressing heavily onto Nash's back.

Inside the store, Nash could hear the frantic clinking of cartridges as Billy reloaded, each metallic sound tightening the noose around his survival. Billy's hands were clumsy, trembling with anger and desperation, but he was making progress, plugging rounds into his revolver as fast as he could manage. Nash fought against Pa's crushing hold, glancing back just in time to see Billy emerge from the doorway, gun raised, his face twisted in fury.

"Billy, don't—!" Pa Oakley shouted, his voice tinged with fear, realizing too late what was about to happen.

But Billy was beyond reason. His hands shook as he aimed, his finger finding the trigger. He fired, the sound cracking through the air. Nash felt the impact before he saw it—Pa Oakley jerked back, a strangled gasp escaping him as he slumped, his grip weakening as his body sagged onto Nash's shoulder.

Nash wasted no time. With one last push, he threw Pa's weight off him and rolled, his fingers scrabbling in the dirt until they found the grip of his Colt. The cold, familiar weight steadied him as he brought it up, leveling it at Billy, who was still standing there, staring at his father's crumpled form in stunned horror.

"Drop it," Nash's steady, low voice was filled with an unrelenting finality. But Billy barely registered it. His face was pale, his eyes wide, and his chest heaved as he struggled to comprehend what he'd done. Billy's hand shifted, moving the gun towards Nash.

Nash squeezed the trigger. The Colt roared, and Billy staggered back, clutching his chest as the bullet struck true. His knees buckled, and he collapsed, the gun slipping from his fingers, his last breath a soft, shocked whisper as he fell still.

Nash exhaled, his hand still gripping the Colt, his breathing ragged as he looked down at the two Oakleys lying in the dirt. The dust settled slowly around them, and the quiet that followed was thick and heavy, carrying the weight of everything that had transpired.

CHAPTER NINETEEN

Alice burst through the doorway of the general store, her boots skidding slightly on the dusty wooden floor as she bolted down the aisle. Her heart pounded as she maneuvered around overturned shelves, scattered cans, and broken crates. Billy Oakley's body lay sprawled outside the back of the shop, his face frozen in a look of stunned disbelief, but she stepped over him without hesitation, barely sparing him a glance.

"Nash!" she called her voice a breathless mixture of worry and relief. She slowed as she reached him, her eyes scanning him for any sign of injury.

Nash looked up, wiping a streak of dust and blood from his cheek. His Colt was still clutched in his hand, smoke curling faintly from the barrel. He straightened as she approached, giving her a reassuring nod.

"Are you okay?" she asked, her voice catching as she took in the scene, the bodies of Pa and Billy Oakley lying lifeless in the dust, and Nash himself, standing in the aftermath with a look of weary determination.

"I'm fine, Alice," Nash replied, his voice steady but rough around the edges, and grinned. "Just finished up here."

Alice's shoulders sagged with relief, but her expression remained urgent. She took a deep breath before speaking, her eyes flashing with worry. "Nash, there's one more left. Ted Oakley's been cornered by Hank. My father's holding him at gunpoint in the alley out back."

Nash's expression sharpened, and he let out a low breath, tucking the Colt into his holster. "Where are they?"

"They're right behind the saloon," Alice said quickly, nodding toward the back door. "Hank found him trying to circle around, probably hoping to ambush you, but he's got him cornered now. I don't know how long he can keep him there."

Nash didn't waste a second. He turned on his heel, gripping Alice's arm as he moved past her toward the door. "Stay close," he murmured, his tone firm but gentle.

Alice nodded, falling in step beside him as they navigated the store's wreckage and headed toward the exit. The cool, stale air inside gave way to the heat of the morning as Nash pushed open the door, revealing the narrow, dusty alley behind the building.

At the far end of the alley, Hank stood, his shotgun trained on Ted Oakley, who was backed up against the wall, his hands held halfway up, defiance and fear mingling in his eyes as he glared at Hank. Blood leaking from the wound where Nash's bullet had caught him earlier.

As Nash and Alice approached, Hank's gaze flicked to them, a grim look of relief crossing his face. "Glad you made it, Nash," he said, his voice steady but filled with tension. "Got this one thinking he could outsmart us, but I reckon he knows better now."

Ted's gaze darted between them, his jaw clenched. "You're all cowards," he spat, his voice dripping with venom. "This ain't over. My pa—"

"Your pa's done, and so is your brother," Nash interrupted, his voice cold and final. He took a slow, measured step forward, meeting Ted's gaze with a steely glare. "And so are you."

Ted hesitated, his hands twitching, but Nash could see the fear flickering in his eyes. Whatever defiance he'd clung to before was quickly draining away, leaving him cornered and outnumbered.

Hank shifted his grip on the gun, his eyes hard as he watched Ted's every move. "If you're smart, Ted, you'll listen to Nash …." He didn't finish, letting the weight of the unfinished sentence hang in the air.

Ted Oakley leaned heavily against the wall, his face pale, blood staining the torn sleeve of his shirt. His defiant expression had faded, replaced by exhaustion and bitterness that seemed to weigh him down as he met Nash's unyielding gaze.

He took a shuddering breath, his voice rough and strained. "Fine," he muttered, wincing as he shifted his injured arm. "I'll leave. You won't see me in Buffalo Gap again."

Nash studied him for a long moment, his eyes hard and unrelenting. "Make sure of it. 'Cause if you come back… next time, there won't be a warning."

Ted clenched his jaw, casting one last look around him—a mixture of anger and regret in his eyes as he glanced at Alice, then Hank, who still held the shotgun at the ready. Without another word, he turned and limped toward his horse. Every step seemed to cost him, his movements slow and labored, his hand pressed against the wound in his arm.

Alice, Nash, and Hank watched in silence as he struggled to pull himself into the saddle, wincing as he finally managed to swing his leg over. His face twisted in pain, and he gripped the reins tightly, leaning forward against the saddle horn for support. He looked back over his shoulder one last time, a bitter scowl twisting his features, before spurring the horse forward.

They stood together, unmoving, as Ted made his way down the dusty main street of Buffalo Gap. The townsfolk peered from behind curtains and cracked doors, watching the last Oakley son ride away, his figure gradually shrinking as he left town. His horse moved at a slow, unsteady pace, Ted slumped forward, clinging to the saddle as he disappeared over the horizon.

Only when he was a distant speck did Hank lower the gun, exhaling a long, tired breath. "Well," he said, looking over at Nash and Alice, a weary relief in his voice, "reckon that's the last of 'em."

Nash nodded, his gaze still fixed on the road, watching until Ted was gone from sight. As the last dust cloud from Ted Oakley's departure settled on the horizon, Nash remained motionless, his gaze still fixed on the vanishing speck. He still felt the weight of Buffalo Gap—the violence, the suspicion, the way the town seemed to cling to its trouble like a second skin. He had hoped that ending the Oakleys' rule might have lifted that burden.

Still, standing there with Hank and Alice, he felt something different stirring within him—a pull he wasn't sure he wanted to name, and one he wasn't sure he liked.

Dropping the Colt back into the holster Nash turned to Alice. He wrapped his arms around her, pulling her close, his heart racing as he leaned down and captured her lips in a kiss that felt like the world had stopped. It was tender, yet full of undeniable passion—a kiss that spoke of unspoken feelings and gratitude tangled together. In that moment, everything else vanished, leaving only the two of them, caught in a moment that would be forever etched in their memories—a kiss to remember.

As they pulled apart, both a little breathless, Nash looked deep into Alice's eyes. "You have no idea how long I've waited for that," he confessed, a playful smile tugging at his lips.

Alice blushed, her shyness momentarily forgotten. "I think I do now," she replied, her voice barely a whisper.

Hank cleared his throat, breaking the silence. Alice blushed and pulled from Nash's embrace. Reluctantly he let her go.

Dropping the Colt back into its holster, Nash turned toward Alice, his rough exterior momentarily softened by the tenderness in his gaze. Without hesitation, he wrapped his arms around her, drawing her close. The world around them seemed to fade into nothingness as he leaned down, capturing her lips in a kiss that carried the weight of unspoken feelings, relief, and gratitude.

The kiss was electric and consuming, tender yet unrestrained, as though it had been waiting to happen for a lifetime. Alice responded without hesitation, her hands resting lightly on his chest before sliding around his neck. For that brief moment, the chaos of Buffalo Gap, the scars of the past, and the uncertainty of the future dissolved, leaving only the two of them—two souls finding solace in each other.

When they finally pulled apart, their breaths mingled in the charged air between them. Nash kept his arms around her, a faint smile playing at the corners of his lips. "You have no idea how long I've waited for that," he said, his voice low and almost teasing, though his words carried a depth that made her heart race.

Alice blushed, a rare mix of shyness and boldness glimmering in her eyes. "I think I do now," she replied softly, her voice barely audible.

The moment lingered, both of them caught in the quiet intimacy of their newfound connection. But just as Nash began to lean in again, savoring the closeness, a loud and deliberate throat-clearing shattered the stillness.

Hank stood a few feet away, arms crossed and one eyebrow raised in a look that managed to be both disapproving and amused. "Well, don't mind me," he said, his tone dry.

Alice pulled back from Nash with a startled laugh, her face turning crimson as she tried to step away. Nash let out a resigned sigh, his hands dropping reluctantly to his sides.

Nash felt a wave of regret settle over him as the moment slipped away. Hank, as stubborn as ever, showed no sign of leaving, his presence an immovable reminder of reality. Alice, her cheeks still flushed with embarrassment, cast a final, apologetic glance over her shoulder before turning leave.

Nash's eyes lingered on her as she walked away, her steps hesitant at first, as though she might turn back. But she didn't. Beside him, Hank's voice droned on, his words lost to the haze of disappointment clouding Nash's mind. Nash barely registered the sound, his thoughts consumed by what had been left unfinished, by what could have been.

Nash walked slowly down the main street, each step deliberate, his boots crunching over gravel and kicking up dust. His shirt was torn, his face bruised, and a streak of blood ran from his temple down to his jaw. One hand rested on his revolver, the other hung limp at his side, the ache in his shoulder a sharp reminder of how close the fight had come to ending him, and another ache in his chest after Alice had slipped from his arms.

He paused, his eyes sweeping the street. Marthe stood outside the saloon, surveying the damage with a mixture of relief and sorrow. A young boy darted past, picking up a discarded hat from the dirt. The general store's shattered windows revealed shelves in disarray, jars and tins scattered across the floor. Despite the wreckage, there was a hum of life. People were talking, moving around without fear – the Oakley's were gone.

Nash continued down the street, his gait stiff but steady. A few townsfolk glanced his way, their faces a mix of gratitude and wariness. He wasn't sure if their looks were for the man who had stood against the Oakleys or the drifter who had brought the storm to their door in the first place. Nash came to a halt near the livery yard. He didn't really know where else to go.

"You standin' there like a statue, or you gonna lend a hand?" Hank's gravelly voice broke Nash's reverie. The older man limped toward him, his shotgun still slung over his shoulder, his expression one of tired amusement.

Nash smiled faintly, rubbing his jaw, he was still annoyed with Hank, but he tried to not let it show. "Figured I'd stay out of the way of the real work."

Hank snorted, glancing toward Alice. "That's fair enough. You did your part. Town owes you for it."

Nash's smile faded as he looked back toward the saloon. Marthe was already directing two men to nail up planking over the broken windows. "Maybe. But I wonder how long it'll be before someone else comes lookin' to stir up trouble. This town feels like it's got a magnet for it."

Hank's gaze narrowed, his tone softening. "Trouble finds every town, Nash.

Question is, do you run from it, or do you stick around to face it?"

Nash didn't answer immediately. The pride he felt for standing up to the Oakleys was tempered by a lingering doubt. Had his presence helped Buffalo Gap—or simply brought more pain to its people? Finally, he sighed, tilting his hat back. "Reckon I'll think on that."

"You do that," Hank said, patting Nash's shoulder lightly before moving off.
Nash stood there for a moment longer, the sun warming his back as the town slowly pieced itself together. He turned when he heard more footfalls coming his way, it was Martha.

"Well, cowboy, it's been quite a day. I've a plate of food for you, and that shoulder needs seeing so and I'm not taking no for an answer, do you hear me?" Martha said smiling as she hooked her arm through his and began to steer him towards the saloon.

"I'll not argue with you, ma'am," Nash replied.

"Nash," Martha said as they walked, her voice soft but steady. "I... I want to thank you, on behalf of myself and my family. Callum always believed in doing what was right, even when it was hard, and yesterday... you did what was right. You gave this town a chance to stand up against the Oakleys when we might've let them tear us apart."

Her voice caught for a moment, and she took a deep breath. "I don't know what comes next for Buffalo Gap, but I know we owe you a debt we can't repay. I hope... I hope you'll stay. This town could use a man like you."

"Ma'am," he said, his voice quiet but clear. "I appreciate your words. Your husband was a good man. Braver than most. What I did... it wasn't for thanks. It was just what needed doin'."

Martha's eyes shone, they'd reached the saloon and there were now a crowd of other townsfolk gathered watching his approach. A young man raised his hand, his voice eager. "We could use someone like you, Nash. Someone who ain't afraid to stand up to folks like the Oakleys. Maybe even as sheriff."

The murmurs grew louder, some voices agreeing, others not so sure. One man near the back stepped forward, his face lined with suspicion. "And what makes us think he'll stick around? He's a drifter. One fight doesn't change that."

Another voice chimed in, sharper. "And what about his Apache blood? Who's to say he ain't just looking for an excuse to cause trouble here?"

The murmurs turned uneasy, shifting in tone. Nash's jaw tightened, but he remained outwardly calm.

Hank, standing nearby, slammed the butt of his shotgun against the ground with a sharp crack, silencing the crowd. "You all better think real careful before you go bitin' the hand that just saved your sorry hides," he growled. "Nash fought for this town when most of you were too scared to. Don't matter where he's from or what blood runs in his veins. He stood with us, and that's more than most."

The tension in the crowd eased slightly, but the wary glances didn't entirely fade. Nash tipped his hat to Hank in silent thanks before addressing the group.

"I ain't here to cause trouble," he said, his voice steady but reserved. "And I ain't lookin' to be anybody's savior. I came to Buffalo Gap passing through, and that's what I am—a man just passing through. I'll lend a hand where I can, but I ain't sure this town is a place I can call home."

The crowd fell silent, some nodding in understanding, others exchanging uneasy looks.

Martha took him by the arm again. "Sometimes a place becomes home when you decide to stay, Nash. This town has a long way to go, but we'd be better off if you were part of it."

Nash met her gaze, his own expression unreadable. "Maybe," he said after a long pause. "But that's somethin' I'll have to think on."

He turned slightly, his eyes scanning the crowd, seeing both the hope and the doubt in their faces. The weight of their gratitude—and their wariness—pressed heavy on him. With a curt nod, he stepped up the steps to the saloon next to Martha, leaving the townsfolk to their conversations, his thoughts a storm of conflict.

Behind him, the voices rose again, some hopeful, some still questioning. Nash wasn't sure if Buffalo Gap could ever be more than a stop on his endless journey. But as he glanced back once, he caught sight of Alice, her steady gaze meeting his from across the street. The smallest hint of a smile tugged at the corner of her lips, and for a fleeting moment, he wondered if staying might not be such a bad idea after all.

Nash ate alone at the back of the saloon , he felt guilty that men were fixing up the saloon around him, that Martha was clearing away broken glass and sweeping the floors, but she'd not let him help. "You've done enough, cowboy," she'd said when he'd tried to.

When he'd finished his meal he slipped out of the back of the saloon and rounded to the livery yard where his horse was. Nash stood by his horse, brushing down her coat with slow, deliberate strokes. The rhythmic motion of the brush was calming, a small ritual in a life otherwise marked by chaos. His saddlebags were packed and resting nearby, a silent testament to his decision to leave Buffalo Gap behind.

He didn't look up when he heard the sound of footsteps behind him. He didn't need to—he already knew it was Alice. Her stride was purposeful but hesitant, her boots crunching softly against the straw-strewn ground.

"Nash," she called softly, her voice carrying both warmth and frustration.
He paused, resting a hand on the horse's flank before turning to face her. She stood a few feet away, her arms crossed, her expression a mix of determination and sadness.

"You're leaving," she said, though it wasn't a question.

Nash nodded, his blue eyes meeting hers. "It's better this way, Alice."

"For who?" she countered, stepping closer. "For you? For the town? Or are you just running again?"

Nash flinched at her words, but his face remained composed. "You've seen what happens when I'm around, Alice. Trouble follows me like a shadow. Buffalo Gap's been through enough. They don't need more of it, and neither do you."

Alice sighed, her hands falling to her sides. "Nash, you're not the one who brought trouble here. The Oakleys were the problem, not you. If it weren't for you, this town wouldn't have survived them."

"And what about the next time?" Nash said, his voice low but firm. "What happens when someone else comes gunning for me? Or someone decides they don't trust the half-Apache drifter who helped clean up their town? I'm not exactly the kind of man folks want to put their faith in."

Alice shook her head, her eyes narrowing with frustration. "You think you're protecting us by leaving? You're wrong. All you're doing is leaving us vulnerable. The Oakleys may be gone, but the world doesn't stop being dangerous just because you've ridden off into the sunset."

Nash turned away, his hand gripping the saddle horn as if steadying himself. "I don't want you caught in that, Alice," he said quietly. "You deserve better than a life of looking over your shoulder, wondering who's coming for me next."

Alice stepped forward, her voice softening but losing none of its conviction. "You think I don't know what I'm choosing, Nash? I've seen the worst of it, stood right beside you through it all. If I wanted to run, I would've done it long before now. But I'm still here, and so are you."

Nash glanced at her, the weight of her words pressing on him. "Alice, I've spent my whole life drifting. Staying in one place... it's not what I'm made for. I don't know how to be anything but a man passing through."

Alice's voice caught slightly, but she pushed on. "Maybe you don't, but that doesn't mean you can't learn. The people here—they need someone like you. Someone who doesn't back down when things get tough. Someone who knows what it means to fight for what's right."

Her words hit him like a blow, and he dropped his gaze, staring at the dirt beneath his boots. "And what about you, Alice? What happens if I stay and it still doesn't work out? What if I can't be the man you need me to be?"

Alice reached out, placing a hand gently on his arm. He didn't pull away. "You don't have to be perfect, Nash. You just have to be here. You've been running so long you've forgotten what it feels like to stand still. Let this be the place you stop running."

For a long moment, silence hung between them. Nash stared at the ground, his thoughts a storm of doubt and longing. Alice's hand remained on his arm, steady and sure, grounding him in a way he hadn't felt in years.

Finally, he exhaled, a sound heavy with resignation and something softer—hope, perhaps. "Alice... I don't know if I can do it. But maybe... maybe it's time I tried."

A small smile tugged at her lips, and she nodded. "Anyway there's a celebration planned in the saloon, you've at least got to stay for that, Martha'll be mad if you don't."

He looked at her then, really looked, and saw the strength and faith in her gaze. For the first time in a long time, he felt like maybe, just maybe, he could belong somewhere. Even if it was only for a little while.

When Nash turned back to his horse, it wasn't because he wanted to; it was because he couldn't trust himself to do what he truly wanted—to pull Alice into his arms. Hank's lingering disapproval weighed on him like a brand.

But then he looked at her—really looked—and saw something in her gaze that stopped him short. Strength. Faith. A quiet assurance that he hadn't seen in a long time. For the first time in what felt like forever, a flicker of hope stirred inside him. Maybe, just maybe, he could belong somewhere. Even if only for a little while.

He ran a hand along his horse's neck, grounding himself. "Guess I'd better unpack those saddlebags, I'm not brave enough to get on the wrong side of Martha, I've seen the lady handle a shotgun," he said, a faint, reluctant smile tugging at his lips.

Alice laughed, the sound warm and light, wrapping around him like a promise. "Guess you should."

CHAPTER TWENTY

The saloon was alive with the sound of laughter and voices, its atmosphere transformed from tense and quiet to warm and welcoming. Lanterns hung from the rafters, casting a golden glow over the room, and the smell of roasted meats and fresh bread filled the air. The townsfolk of Buffalo Gap, battered but resilient, gathered to celebrate their survival—a hard-fought victory that wouldn't have been possible without Nash.

Nash stood by the wall near the back of the room, arms crossed, his battered hat tipped low to shield his face from the attention. He wasn't one for crowds, and the idea of being at the center of this gathering made his shoulders tighten. Yet, he couldn't bring himself to leave. The sound of Alice's laugh carried through the room, and his eyes instinctively sought her out. She was moving between tables, smiling warmly as she passed out drinks, her presence a calming force amidst the boisterous crowd.

Hank, standing by the bar, tapped a spoon against his whiskey glass, the sharp clang cutting through the noise. The room gradually quieted, and all eyes turned to him. Hank, steady and unflappable as ever, cleared his throat and surveyed the room.

"Folks," he began, his voice carrying the weight of authority and warmth. "We've been through hell these past few weeks. The Oakleys tore through this town like a wildfire, and we nearly lost everything. But we're still here. And there's one man who's the reason for that."

He turned his gaze to Nash, nodding toward him. "Nash," Hank called, his voice firm but kind, "come on up here."

The room shifted, all eyes falling on Nash. He hesitated, his instinct screaming to stay put, but Alice appeared beside him, her hand gently brushing his arm. "Go on," she whispered, her voice soft but encouraging. "They want to thank you."

With a reluctant sigh, Nash pushed off the wall and walked toward Hank, his boots scuffing against the wooden floor. The crowd parted for him, murmurs of gratitude rippling through the room as he passed. He stopped next to Hank, adjusting the brim of his hat as he looked out at the faces staring back at him.

"This man," Hank said, gesturing toward Nash, "stood up when no one else would. He faced the Oakleys head-on, knowing full well the risk. He saved lives. He saved this town. And I reckon it's time we showed him what that means to us."

A murmur of agreement swept through the room, and one by one, people began to stand. Callum's widow was the first, her voice trembling with emotion. "You gave us hope, Nash. When my husband was killed, I thought all was lost. But you stood up for us, and I'll never forget it."

Next, it was the wheelright, a burly man with a weathered face. "You've got grit,

Nash. Guts, too. You didn't have to stay and fight, but you did. And for that, you've got my respect."

Even Clem, who'd been one of Nash's harshest critics, rose to his feet. "Reckon I was wrong about you," Clem admitted, his voice gruff. "Didn't think much of a drifter like you, but you proved me wrong. This town owes you, and I won't forget that."

The room erupted in applause, the sound reverberating off the saloon walls. Nash shifted uncomfortably under the weight of their gratitude, his hand brushing against the revolver at his hip—a reminder of the life he'd led up until now.

When the noise settled, Hank spoke again, his voice steady. "Buffalo Gap's seen a lot of men come and go. But Nash, you've shown us what it means to stand tall when it matters most. If you'll stay, I reckon this town could use someone like you."

The crowd murmured in agreement, nodding and offering smiles of encouragement. Nash looked down at his boots, the words catching in his throat. For so long, he'd been a drifter, a man with no ties and no place to call home. The idea of staying, of putting down roots, felt as foreign as it was tempting.

He glanced at Alice, standing near the bar, her hands clasped in front of her as she watched him with quiet hope. Her presence steadied him, gave him a reason to consider what he might gain if he stayed.

Finally, Nash cleared his throat, looking out at the expectant faces around him.

"I appreciate what you're saying," he began, his voice low but clear. "But I ain't sure if I'm the kind of man who can settle down. My life's been... complicated. And trouble has a way of finding me."

Hank placed a reassuring hand on his shoulder. "Ain't nobody here who doesn't have their own troubles, Nash. But you've shown us what kind of man you are. If you're willing to give Buffalo Gap a chance, I reckon we'll do the same for you."

The room was silent, the weight of Hank's words hanging in the air. Nash looked out at the crowd again, at the faces of people who, for the first time in his life, seemed to truly see him—not as a half-Apache drifter, but as a man who had made a difference.

"I'll think on it," Nash finally said, his words met with a ripple of approval. The townsfolk clapped again, their applause genuine and heartfelt.

As the celebration continued, Nash slipped back to his place near the wall, the noise of the room fading as his thoughts took over. For the first time in a long time, he felt something stir within him—hope, perhaps, or the faintest sense of belonging. He wasn't sure yet if he'd stay, but for the first time, the idea didn't seem so impossible.

Nash stayed on, working in the livery yard under Hank's watchful eye. The work was hard, honest, and gave him little time to dwell on his tangled thoughts. Weeks passed, and though he and Hank kept things civil, there was a distance between them that neither seemed eager to bridge.

One evening, just as Nash was brushing down one of the geldings, Hank appeared at the edge of the stall. His hat was in his hands, fingers worrying the brim—a sign, Nash figured, that the man was as uneasy about the conversation as he was.

Hank cleared his throat. "Got a minute?"

Nash paused, setting the brush aside. "Sure."

Hank stepped inside, glancing around like the words he was about to say might be overheard by someone other than the horse. "Look, I ain't good at this kind of thing, but... if I've given you the impression you're not to court Alice, that wasn't my intention."

Nash blinked, caught off guard. "I wasn't sure how you felt about it."

"Well," Hank went on, clearly uncomfortable, "it's just, she's been pretty down lately. Said you've been ignoring her. Thought maybe I ought to say something, in case that's got anything to do with me."

Nash frowned and leaned back against the stall door, arms crossed. "I might've kissed her. Gave her the wrong idea about me. That's why I've been keeping my distance. Didn't want her thinking..." He trailed off, unsure how to explain the storm of doubts and fears in his chest.

Hank looked at him for a long moment, then sighed, his cheeks coloring. "Well, hell. Ain't none of my business what you think she might've gotten out of it. But if you're asking me if I'm okay with you not ignoring her anymore—yeah, I am. That's okay by me."

Nash studied the older man, searching for any hint of lingering disapproval. There wasn't any, just a flicker of genuine concern, maybe even hope, in Hank's expression.

"All right," Nash said slowly. "I appreciate you saying so."

Hank nodded, shifting his hat back onto his head. "Guess I'll leave you to it, then."

As Hank walked away, Nash leaned against the stall and exhaled. He wasn't sure what he was going to say to Alice, but one thing was clear: he couldn't keep pretending she didn't matter.

EPILOGUE

The soft sounds of rustling hay and the occasional snort of a horse filled the barn as Nash worked, his shirt damp with sweat from the midday sun streaming through the slats in the walls. His sleeves were rolled up, exposing his tanned forearms as he hefted a pitchfork, spreading fresh straw in the stalls. The faint scent of leather and horses lingered in the air, mingling with the earthy aroma of the barn.

He paused for a moment, wiping his brow with the back of his hand, when the creak of the barn door made him glance up. Alice stepped inside, her figure framed by the golden light. She carried a small basket in her hands, her smile soft and warm as she approached.

"I thought you might be hungry," she said, holding up the basket. "Figured you've been working yourself half to death in here all morning."

Nash leaned the pitchfork against the wall, a slow smile spreading across his face. "You figured right. But I'm not so sure food's what I'm hungry for."

Alice's cheeks flushed a delicate pink, but she didn't look away. "Oh, is that so?" she teased, setting the basket down on a bale of hay.

Before she could say another word, Nash closed the distance between them in a few long strides. His calloused hands found her waist, lifting her easily as if she weighed nothing at all. Alice gasped, half-laughing, as he carried her across the barn and laid her gently onto the soft pile of hay.

"Nash!" she protested playfully, but the glint in her eyes betrayed her excitement.

He leaned over her, his blue eyes intense but warm, his expression softened by the crooked smile playing on his lips. "What?" he asked, his voice a low rumble. "This seems like a mighty fine place to take a break."

Alice laughed softly, her hands resting on his shoulders. "You're impossible."

"Maybe," he replied, leaning down until their foreheads nearly touched. "But you don't seem to mind."

Their eyes locked, and the playful air between them gave way to something deeper. Nash cupped her face in his hands, his thumb brushing her cheek as he brought his lips to hers. The kiss was slow and deliberate at first, but it deepened quickly, carrying the weight of weeks of longing unspoken between them. Alice's arms wrapped around his neck, pulling him closer as the world outside the barn seemed to fade away. Nash's hands slid to her waist, holding her securely as he shifted his weight, pressing them deeper into the soft hay. His kisses trailed from her lips to her jawline, then to the curve of her neck, sending a shiver through her.

"Nash," she whispered, her voice breathless and filled with emotion.

He paused, pulling back just enough to look into her eyes, his hand still cradling her face. "Alice," he murmured, his voice rough but tender. "Tell me to stop if you want me to. Otherwise, I'm not gonna."

Alice shook her head, her fingers threading through his dark hair. "Don't stop," she whispered, her voice steady despite the quickened beat of her heart. "Not ever."

Nash smiled then, a rare, genuine smile that softened the hard lines of his face. He leaned down again, capturing her lips in another kiss, this one filled with a fierce, unspoken promise. Their bodies pressed together, their movements slow and deliberate as they gave in to the passion that had been building between them for so long.

The barn, usually filled with the sounds of creaking wood and restless horses, was now a haven for their shared moment, as they found comfort and belonging in each other's arms. In that quiet, sunlit space, nothing else mattered but the connection they'd found— one as natural and unyielding as the earth beneath them.

Next in the series (free to read on Kindle Unlimited)

The Silent Gunfighter – Book 3

The End

The Silent Gunfighter – Book 3

ALSO BY WYATT STEELE

The Gunfighters Law

TRAIL OF THE GUNFIGHTER SERIES

VENDETTA RIDE – THE WRATH OF
WYATT EARP

THE OUTLAW McCOY SERIES

DRIFTER GRITTY WESTERN SERIES

Printed in Dunstable, United Kingdom

70231115R10102